Rabbit-

Go-Lucky

By PHYLLIS N. COTÉ

Illustrated by the Author

JUNIOR BOOKS

Doubleday, Doran & Company, Inc.

GARDEN CITY, NEW YORK

PRINTED AT THE *Country Life Press*, GARDEN CITY, N. Y., U. S. A.

THIS BOOK IS
STANDARD LENGTH,
COMPLETE AND UNABRIDGED,
MANUFACTURED UNDER WARTIME CONDITIONS
IN CONFORMITY WITH ALL GOVERNMENT
REGULATIONS CONTROLLING THE USE
OF PAPER AND OTHER MATERIALS

RABBIT-GO-LUCKY

To Ricks
from
Mary and Paul

To MOTHER and DADDY and DICK
(how could I choose just one?)
this book is affectionately dedicated.

———————

My sincere thanks to Miss Edith Fetteroff and Mrs. Jay Hambidge for their generous information concerning reels and rabbits.

Come luck, come light, my spinning,
Come soft and warm, my web;
Sings the rippling laughing water
Work is but grown-up play.
Sings the rippling laughing water
Work is but grown-up play.

New verse for an old folk song

Contents

CHAPTER   PAGE

I   Doldrums 9

II   Back-Yard Barbershop 25

III Merry Spinster 41

IV Wheels and Reels 64

V   Indian Pudding Party 82

VI Whistlin' Amy Adams 96

VII Ring Around the Moon 113

VIII Thunder Bird 126

IX Beehive 141

X   Saturday Jamboree 159

I

Doldrums

"I PACKED my trunk for Paris," chanted Mary Jane MacGregor as she dangled idly on the back-yard swing, "and in it I put an apple, a bear, and a—a candle! Your turn, Sandy," she called to her young brother, who was near by busily chopping up a bunch of fresh carrots for his rabbits' supper. He had propped a pair of wooden crates under each end of the long seesaw and was using it now as a worktable.

"I packed my trunk for Paris," said Sandy, "and in it I put an apple, a bear, a candle, and a—and——" He stopped for a moment and screwed up his eyes to think of something that started with a "d." His real name was Alexander, and he was nine. His brown freckled face was topped by a wild thatch of short red hair. ("I declare," Mother used to say when she tried to part it, "no two hairs on your head grow in the same direction!") Sandy had on a rumpled yellow polo shirt, tails flying, and old white ducks with the cuffs rolled up, exposing his bramble-scratched legs and grass-stained sneakers. At last his brow cleared and he exclaimed triumphantly, "And a derrick!"

"Sandy," Mary Jane asked suddenly, "what would you really do with those things?"

"I don't know," answered Sandy, lopping the green feathery top off another carrot. "Eat the apple, I guess, and I'd tame the old bear, and I'd put the candle in our camp out in the woods. But, boy, what fun I'd have with that derrick! What would you do with them?" he asked with brotherly interest.

"I'd give them all away," Mary Jane said fiercely, "and then I'd *really* pack my trunk for Paris!"

She was tall for eleven, with long amber-colored hair that hung to her slim shoulders. Already she had almost outgrown the blue-and-white pinafore she was wearing, which was brand new just last spring. Her small, intense face was lit with deep brown eyes, now dangerously close to tears. She dug at the scuffed earth below the swing with the toe of her sandaled foot.

Sandy didn't look up, but he stopped chopping and stood very still, with a strange feeling in the pit of his stomach.

"Why do you want to go away, Mary Jane?" he asked.

The late afternoon sun flickered through the leaves of

the apple tree, but Mary Jane, under the largest bough, was in shadows.

"Because I'm sick and tired of always living in New Hampshire, that's why!" she cried with a rush of pent-up feeling. "Lucky Ellen's gone to camp, and Nancy's at the beach. But I have to go right on staying here, with those great green hills all around, shutting me in with nothing to do. Nothing to do the whole summer long but make my bed and set the table, and eat and sleep, and weed the garden for Daddy if I want a dime, and watch the baby when Mother's away. Oh dear, I almost wish school would start again. At least it keeps you from wondering what to do."

"Don't wish that!" Sandy interrupted hastily, as though afraid that, if Mary Jane wished hard enough, it might happen. "We just got out of that place. Gosh, I thought June'd *never* come."

"Well," she maintained, restlessly jerking the heavy, worn rope of the swing, "I'd still like to pack my trunk for Paris—or London or Brazil or any place."

"But, Mary Jane," said Sandy slowly, looking at his sister with troubled eyes, "no matter where you go in the world, yourself goes too. If you don't like it in New Hampshire, how do you know you'd like it any better in Paris or London or Brazil?"

"I don't know. I'd just like to try it, that's all," Mary Jane answered. "There's no fun around here."

"I like it," declared Sandy stoutly as he scooped up the chopped carrots to put them into the three glazed earthenware bowls. "I like it fine."

"That's on account of your rabbits," said Mary Jane, turning toward the sturdy wooden pens surrounded by a hedge of tall yellow sunflowers which stood like a gay rack of open umbrellas, protecting the rabbits from too much wind or sun.

It was true. Sandy lived and breathed for his three Angora rabbits that had been given to him last Easter by Uncle Toby, who owned a big farm down in Londonderry. Daddy, who was Uncle Toby's youngest brother, used to raise rabbits himself when he was a boy on that very same farm, so he taught Sandy how to take care of his rabbits. He showed him the way their long, fine fur had to be brushed and told him what vegetables they liked best and how to fix them. With the help of Ebenadams, the remarkable old man next door, Sandy built the rabbit hutch out of some lumber the carpenters left when they built the MacGregors' new two-stalled garage. The pens were raised on little stilts so they wouldn't be damp or drafty, and the wire netting, stretched on wooden frames that fenced off the play yard, was set deep in the ground so the frisky rabbits couldn't burrow under and run away.

"Rabbits do take most of my time," Sandy admitted cheerfully. "Say, they'd sure love some celery in with these carrots. . . . Where's Mother?"

"She went to an auction in Candia with Mrs. Wyman," said Mary Jane.

"Hmph, more antiques!" said Sandy, being just like a man.

"She doesn't buy only antiques," defended Mary Jane. "Last time she bought some hand-hooked rugs. And once she got five jars of wild strawberry jam at an auction, remember?"

"That's right—there's no telling *what* she might bring home. Wonder what it'll be today?" Sandy mused as he broke a carrot top into delicate little sprigs for extra flavor. "When will she be back?"

"Any time now," answered Mary Jane. "Besides, that celery is for *our* supper, not——"

"Ding-ding-ding-ding-ding!" clanged a little boy charging into the yard at full speed, flashing by in his red corduroy overalls like a midget fire engine. Two surprised robins flickered hurriedly out of his way.

"Where's the fire?" grinned Sandy.

"All out!" panted the little fellow, wheeling around and stopping short at his big brother's side. "I like carrots a lot," he said, peering on tiptoe into the rabbits' dishes. Good-naturedly, Sandy scraped an extra carrot for him.

Nearly four years ago, when Mother brought home their baby brother for the first time, she had gently pulled aside the downy blue blanket so that Mary Jane and Sandy could see what a funny little elf he was, with his coal-black hair and solemn black eyes.

"What's his name?" Sandy had asked.

"Mark," said Daddy.

"Ditto Mark!" laughed Mary Jane. "Because he looks just like you, only he came in the smallest size."

So ever since then Mark MacGregor was known as Ditto.

"Where are your shoes?" asked Mary Jane, suddenly noticing that Ditto was padding around in his stocking feet. He had on white hand-knit socks with colored toes. Mother always used her odds and ends of colored yarns for toes.

"I took them off," said Ditto matter-of-factly, crunching the raw sweet carrot Sandy handed him.

"So I see. . . . Where did you put them?"

With Mother away Mary Jane was "top sergeant" for the afternoon and therefore responsible for the whereabouts of Ditto and his belongings.

"I took them off," he remembered, swallowing with a

little gulp in order to talk. "And I put one shoe on the curbstone and I put one shoe under the magnolia tree."

"What did you do that for?" questioned Sandy.

"Because shoes can never go anywhere *alone*," he explained gravely. "When they're *on*, they both have to go together to the same places. They always do, unless you take them *off*."

"Oh, Ditto," groaned Mary Jane, "shoes are *supposed* to go together in pairs. Now you go get them and put them on this minute."

"Hurry up," Sandy called after Ditto as he obligingly trudged off. "It's nearly time to feed the rabbits."

By the time Ditto's shoes were recovered and his shoestrings securely tied by Mary Jane, Sandy had the three

bowls filled with chopped carrots, a few carrot tops, and a sprinkling of sunflower seeds.

"Let's each take one," he suggested. "This is for Frosting, Mary Jane, and here, Ditto, you can take Feather's supper to her if you're careful not to spill any."

Feather and Frosting were the two little furry white sisters who lived in the same pen. Sandy himself would carry the third bowl to their brother Polar, the large white rabbit who lived in a pen of his own.

Feeding the rabbits was fun. Feather scampered down the straw-strewn runway when she saw her supper coming, and Frosting already had her wiggling little nose pressed through the wire netting. Polar's short, tufted ears stood up at attention like two white plumes. They all acted as eager and hungry as though they hadn't eaten for days. Usually they nibbled away on the fresh, clean straw in their pens whenever they felt like it, so weren't especially hungry at supper time—although, round healthy rabbits that they were, they were always ready and willing to eat some more.

"They can hardly wait," chuckled Ditto, down on all fours.

"Good thing their dishes have the edges turned in," observed Sandy. "They can't scratch the food out, no matter what kind of a hurry they're in to get a bite.

"There you are, Polar boy, tuck that under your belt," he invited as he unlatched the door of the pen and placed the dish inside. Polar immediately began to relish the toothsome carrots with gusto. "Does that tickle his palate!" said Sandy, as gratified as a mother hen over the good appetite of one of her chicks.

"Look at those bunnies gobble!" shouted Ditto with delight, banging his head against the netting.

"Shsh, let them eat," warned Sandy, pulling him away. All three MacGregors, kneeling back on the grass, watched in silence.

The door of the larger pen was open, and Mary Jane, bending forward, let her fingers slide along Feather's warm, plump back. "She's as soft as smoke," she whispered.

"Nice and shiny, too, with the sunlight on her coat like that," Sandy said proudly. His arm was still tired from the most recent brushing. "Can you reach their pans, Mary Jane? I've got to get them some fresh water."

As Mary Jane lifted up the enamel pans and handed them to Sandy, who already had Polar's, the rumble of a car was heard in the driveway. They waited expectantly. Sure enough—there was the cheery and familiar "Toot-toot!" of a horn.

"Mother's home!" shrieked Ditto, stumbling to his

feet. "And something big's tied onto the top of the car!" he exclaimed as it came into view.

"Golly, look at that, will you!" Sandy grabbed Ditto's hand and gave him a tug. "Come on!" he urged, running toward the car laden like a gypsy's. "Come on!"

Mary Jane picked up the scattered water pans, forgotten in the excitement of Mother's arrival, and slowly followed after.

"Hi, Mother! What have you got?" called Sandy.

"Is it a bed? Is it a bed, Mama?" asked Ditto, eying the top of the car, which was covered with an old patchwork quilt to prevent its strange wooden cargo from scratching the finish.

The gaily colored ends of the quilt were fluttering, and so was Ditto's heart, with the hope that this odd contraption might turn out to be a bed, blanket and all, for himself. He scorned his babyish crib and would have refused to sleep in it if he didn't unfortunately always fall asleep first.

"Is it a bed?" Ditto asked again.

"Whoa there—just a minute!" pleaded Mother with twinkling eyes and a pleasant laugh. She got out of the car and put the keys in her pocketbook. "No, dear, it's not a bed. It's a present for Mary Jane."

Mary Jane pricked up her ears and stared at the wooden

frame with quickened interest. Even though it did belong to her, she didn't know what it was either.

"First," said Mother, "let's get my new footstool out of our way. It's in the back seat and really a gem."

She pulled it out with Sandy's help—an old mahogany footstool with carved roses on its curving legs. It was upholstered in stiff, scratchy horsehair with several tears. To Sandy it looked neither new nor like a gem, but he didn't want to contradict.

"It's in perfect condition," said Mother. "Just needs to be refinished and polished and reupholstered. I'm going to start some needlepoint right away. Put it in the garage, will you, Sandy? We'll keep it there till we're ready for it."

"Sure thing," said Sandy, eager to get this footstool business over with and find out about the object on top.

"Put it in a nice safe place," said Mother, and added in a pay-attention-please voice, "No one is to touch that footstool—right?"

"Right!" chorused the three MacGregors, mentally tagging the footstool with a "Hands Off" sign.

Mr. Whipple across the street, who left his car outdoors in summer, planned to rent the second stall of the MacGregors' garage when winter came. Meanwhile that second stall made an ideal storing place for skis, sleds, bicycles, garden tools, and Mother's unfinished antiques.

"There!" exclaimed Mother, pulling off her straw hat and running her fingers through her rich red-brown hair, the very color of autumn oak leaves. "Shall we tackle this now or wait till Daddy comes home to help us?"

"Now!" they cried impatiently. "Let's take it off now and see what it is."

"We'll have to do it very carefully," said Mother. "Better untie the knots in these ropes first."

"But, Mama, what *is* it?" wailed Ditto, tugging at her skirts.

"Why, it's a loom!" said Mother, pretending she thought they knew all the time.

"What's a loom?" asked Ditto.

"A loom for what?" asked Sandy.

"A loom for weaving," said Mother.

"But I don't need to weave anything," Mary Jane said in surprise.

Weaving sounded like a lot of work, and more work in an already dull summer wasn't a pleasant prospect. A loom certainly wasn't the sort of a present she'd ever pick out. In fact, it wasn't her idea of a present at all.

"Just wait till you know how," mother smiled as she loosened one of the knots. "Steady, Sandy!"

With Sandy and Mary Jane on one side, pulling the

quilt toward them while Mother, on the opposite running
board, was pushing it, they eased the loom to the edge of
the car top. Thus they managed to move the loom from
its perch. With infinite care they stood it up in the driveway and viewed it curiously from all angles as Mother
folded the quilt.

The loom was smaller than they had supposed. Spare
and compact it stood, with its edges worn smooth, as if it
had been used often before yet was still as hardy and dura-
ble as ever. The upper part of it rested on a table top sup-
ported by sturdy legs, and there were two long, narrow

pedals below. The whole thing was neatly made of honey-colored maple.

"It's a lot of rigging for girl-stuff," commented Sandy, who supposed a pair of knitting needles was the most a girl could handle.

"Girl-stuff nothing!" said Mother. "You're going to help in this weaving too."

"*I* am?" Sandy questioned wildly. "Golly, what can *I* do about weaving?"

"Supply the wool," said Mother mysteriously.

Sandy was completely baffled for a moment and then suddenly grinned from ear to ear. "My rabbits!" he whooped. "We're going to give 'em a haircut!"

"Good boy!" approved Mother of Sandy's guess. "Think of the lovely Angora wool you'll have to work with, Mary Jane!"

Mary Jane nodded her head. That much, at least, was true, she thought, remembering the feel of Feather's soft fur in her fingers.

II

Back-Yard Barbershop

THE very next Saturday afternoon, promptly at two, the MacGregors' house was booming with a jolly "Anybody home?" It seemed to come from the back hall, along with the sound of shuffling feet.

Mary Jane, who was drying the dinner dishes, gladly tossed aside the sopping dish towel and called, "They're here!" to her mother, who was upstairs changing her dress.

"Hello, Uncle Toby!" she greeted the large man with ruddy cheeks who by now had made his way into the kitchen. He was carrying a big brown paper bag of vegetables in his robust arms which were covered with little bristling blond hairs from working outdoors in the sun. "Come on in," she said to Aunt Alice, who was following in his wake.

"Whew!" Uncle Toby puffed, putting down his bulky bundle on the kitchen table. "How's my best girl?" he asked, kissing Mary Jane on the ear.

"Fine, thank you," she smiled. "Hello, Aunt Alice."

Aunt Alice gave her a hug and tucked a little white bag into her hand. "It's homemade butter taffy," she said. "Your grandmother's favorite recipe."

"Oh, thank you!" exclaimed Mary Jane, opening the bag. "Have some?"

"Well, maybe just one—to sample it," said Aunt Alice, who couldn't resist whenever her sweet tooth was tempted. She helped herself to one of the chunky nuggets wrapped in waxed paper like candy kisses.

"She sampled it all the way up from Londonderry," teased Uncle Toby, with a wink at Mary Jane.

"Now, Toby, you know I didn't!" said Aunt Alice indignantly. "Why, hello, Helen dear; you're looking splendid!" she cried, delighted to see Mother, in her fresh print dress, come into the room just then.

"Hello, Alice and Toby," said Mother. "It's good to see you again." Then, spotting the huge bundle they brought her, she said, "Oh, you shouldn't have! Not that we don't love them—no one in this world grows vege-tables the way you do!"

"Fiddlesticks!" Uncle Toby scoffed modestly, but well pleased in spite of himself. "Look who's here—if it isn't old Ditto MacGregor himself!"

Ditto, still half asleep from his interrupted nap, wandered in with a drowsy yawn. Blinking at the company, he politely held out his hand and said in one solemn breath, "How-do-you-do-Aunt-Alice-how's-your-chickens?"

"He's a *doll!*" exclaimed Aunt Alice to Mother, snatching up Ditto and smothering him with kisses. "Just a doll!" Aunt Alice originally came from New York City, and, though she had lived in Londonderry for seventeen years, she never had quite acquired Londonderry ways. Ditto, wide awake at once, squirmed in her arms till she was obliged to put him down. He scuttled off without even waiting to hear how the chickens were.

"Don't mind Ditto," said Mary Jane, who privately couldn't understand why anyone who loved fun as much as Aunt Alice would ever leave New York City to live in New Hampshire; though Aunt Alice often said it suited her to live in a state where the people, while thrifty, were not sparing when it came to the table. They liked good food and plenty of it.

"Where are the rest of your menfolk?" questioned Uncle Toby after Ditto darted through the back door.

"Daddy and Sandy are outside, brushing the rabbits," volunteered Mary Jane.

"Already?" said Uncle Toby. "We'll have to get a move on, then, in order to lend them a hand with the clipping. We're going to reap a-plenty for that loom of yours!"

The loom had been put upstairs in Mary Jane's room. It was the first thing she saw in the morning when she opened her eyes, always there to remind her of the weaving work she would soon have to be doing. It was as troubling as a stack of unfinished homework.

Mary Jane and Uncle Toby started out together. Mother and Aunt Alice, chattering away, followed them onto the shady back porch, where they settled themselves in the hammock. The lawn was vividly green in the sunshine of a cloudless sky, and the gardens were buzzing with the lazy drone of black-and-yellow bumblebees.

Mary Jane sat down on the back steps. Reaping a-plenty for that loom of hers didn't interest her. It's just an excuse, she thought rebelliously, for Sandy to have even *more* fun with his rabbits. Idly she looked for the "lady" in the middle of a purple pansy. Its velvety petals lay scattered in her lap like shreds of royal ribbon.

Mother got out the flowered needlepoint which she had just begun for her antique footstool. Aunt Alice, however, left the heavy woolen sweater she was making in her knitting bag.

"It's really too hot for that," she sighed, fanning her face with a handkerchief. "My, how nice and cool those rabbits are going to feel after having their hair cut!"

"Getting a good start, I see," complimented Uncle Toby as he approached the rabbit hutch, where Daddy and Sandy, both in overalls, were sitting on old camp-stools, each brushing a docile rabbit on a little wooden stand in front of him.

"Glad to see you, Toby," said Daddy, looking up. He whistled a greeting at Aunt Alice, who was waving hello with her handkerchief from the porch.

"Hi, Uncle Toby," said Sandy, stopping to brush back his red hair. "What do you hear from Don and Doug?"

"They're both fine and happy as larks," declared Uncle Toby. Cousins Don and Doug went to high school. This vacation, for the first time, instead of working on their father's farm, they had gotten themselves caddying jobs at a summer hotel in the White Mountains. Sandy followed their careers with much interest and admiration.

"Do you have another brush?" asked Uncle Toby, taking off his suit coat and rolling up his shirt sleeves. "I can commence on Feather here, while you two finish Polar and Frosting." Feather and Uncle Toby were old friends.

Sandy handed Uncle Toby the extra brush, and he was soon hard at work, with Feather placed on her stand in front of him. He began by brushing her coat all over with light, easy strokes, first downward and then upward, to get rid of the straw and dust she had picked up in her pen while playing. Then he made a part in the soft wool that extended from the nape of her neck right down to her tail, and brushed downward on both sides with a slight upward sweep, until her wool was clean to the skin where it was parted. He made another part just below the first part and brushed as before, keeping it up, parting and brushing, parting and brushing, until at last Feather's whole coat was groomed and gleaming like silk.

Sandy, meanwhile, was brushing Polar's neck, the hardest part of a rabbit to brush. First he felt around for mats below Polar's cheeks on both sides, teasing the mats out, when he found a few, with his fingers. The finer the hair, the more easily it matted, even though Sandy

brushed his rabbits nearly every day. He gently pulled Polar's ears forward with his left hand and, with a small brush in his right, completed his task. Sandy knew the secret of a soft brush and a loving touch.

After he had finished Frosting, Daddy went into the garage to get the scissors. Sandy, who loved the testing part best, blew on her wool to make sure that there was no cobwebbing and that all the mats were gone. Wherever he blew, Frosting's wool separated easily and he could see her clean pink skin. Daddy had done a most satisfactory job.

Because they had had the rabbits only since Easter the MacGregors had never seen how they were clipped. Uncle Toby said they would need four haircuts a year. Mother and Aunt Alice and Mary Jane came over to the rabbit hutch to watch; and Ditto, who had been off on business of his own, digging up earthworms for the robins, popped up from nowhere the very moment the excitement began.

Uncle Toby bowed to his wide-eyed audience and pretended to doff a tall silk hat, like the master of ceremonies in a three-ring circus. "Ladies and gentlemen," he drawled impressively, "we are here today to witness a performance that is a miracle of manual dexterity. So daring is it that these remarkable rabbits will escape only by a very close shave, or, I should say, haircut. At present they are, as you can see, all snugly blanketed in their fur coats. They don't keep calendars, so they don't realize that the month of July is already upon us and that it's high time to remove their wraps. Otherwise they'd do it for themselves and save us the trouble. Or maybe they just kind of enjoy going to the barbershop and having a haircut—I do myself. Anyhow, Step Number One is to measure the length of their hair." So saying, Uncle Toby closely examined Polar's fur and plucked two or three hairs from it by the roots.

"But you took just the longest ones!" objected Sandy, whose sharp eyes hadn't missed a trick.

"Righto, m'lad!" said Uncle Toby. "You see, a rabbit's wool is always judged by the longest hairs on his body."

"And the short ones don't matter," Sandy said thoughtfully. "Gosh, that's a great idea! Wish they counted only your hundreds in school and skipped all your lower marks."

"The rule, alas, reverses itself when applied to people," said Uncle Toby. "Rabbits are privileged characters."

Skillfully, although his hands were large and his fingers calloused, Uncle Toby laid one of Polar's hairs full length on a flat metal ruler. It measured three and one half inches.

Feather's and Frosting's each measured three.

"Good, good!" muttered Uncle Toby, satisfied. "Now we're ready to begin."

Precisely at that moment Tildy, Ebenadams' peppery housekeeper, came out to take in the washing. Ebenadams' old white clapboard house, with its dilapidated dull-red barn spired with lightning rods and weather-beaten shed of silvery shingles, had been built on top of a hill between two great elms and a few rock maples. Long ago it had been a thriving farm with fertile pastures and a flourishing apple orchard where now a row of houses stood. A gentle green slope divided Ebenadams' land from the MacGregors', and it was on this slope that Tildy was standing with a couple of clothespins in her mouth. She glanced over toward the MacGregors' and, for the life of her, couldn't imagine what was going on.

"Here we go," said Uncle Toby as once more Polar's shiny thick hair was parted from the nape of his neck down to his tail. Daddy handed Uncle Toby a pair of sharp scissors which had blunt ends. Starting at the base of Polar's tail, Uncle Toby clipped a thin line of wool up to Polar's shoulder. By taking his time, he clipped as closely as possible, and was careful to keep the blades level to the surface he was clipping, so Polar wouldn't get cut. Clip-clip petty-clip-clip went the shears, as line after line of snowy white wool fell to the clean brown paper spread out on Polar's stand.

Everyone watched intently, including Tildy, straining her neck from where she stood. Suddenly Ditto, darting out between Mary Jane and Sandy, whirled himself dizzily round and round and round, waving his arms till his little red-and-white-striped jersey was just a pinkish blur.

"Hey, Ditto, hold still!" called Sandy, afraid that so much unexpected motion might frighten Polar during his haircut.

"Take it easy, young fellow!" warned Daddy, perplexed by his twirling son.

"Ditto MacGregor, what *are* you doing?" Mother asked worriedly.

"I'm a barber pole—a barber pole!" he cried, still spinning like a top. "A barber pole!" Couldn't they *see* his red and white stripes going around?

At that they laughed uproariously. Aunt Alice, so weak from laughter that she had to go back on the porch to sit down, gasped as soon as she could, "Just a doll! Just a doll!" Mary Jane and Daddy hung on to Ditto while he "undizzied," and Sandy, chuckling, turned back toward Uncle Toby, whose powerful frame was shaking with deep-throated laughter.

Tildy, more bewildered than ever, still looked on. All the dry clothes were folded away in her basket, yet there she was, in her blue house dress and white apron with rickrack trimming, fussing with an empty clothesline. Tildy was a tall woman with long, thin arms and legs. Her hair was brown and sparse, parted in the middle and looped down over her ears, making her long, narrow face resemble a Gothic window. Her hazel eyes sparkled like colored glass with the sun shining through. Because it was simply beneath her dignity to ask the MacGregors outright just what was going on—but beyond her curiosity to go back into the house without finding out—Tildy kept silent, helplessly rooted to the spot where she stood.

Mother, sensing her predicament, stepped across the lawn and waved. "Hello there, Tildy!"

"Good afternoon," replied Tildy. "Nice day."

"Yes, isn't it," said Mother. "We're really enjoying it out here—watching Sandy's rabbits get a haircut," she added kindly and clearly.

"Indeed," said Tildy without a sign of surprise. "Who'd you say was cutting it?"

"Uncle Toby from Londonderry," answered Mother, "and that's his wife, Aunt Alice, sitting on the porch."

"Well, what do you know!" declared Tildy, pleased to have her mind settled on that point.

"Where's Ebenadams?" Mother inquired in her neigh-borly way. "I haven't seen him once today."

"Oh, Mister Adams is over on t'other side of the house hoein' his potato patch. Been at it all afternoon. I tell him he'd ought to ease up a bit—a man of his age—but he won't listen. Jest says he feels fine and dandy and fer me to stop pesterin' him. Heavens to Betsey, the way he takes on when a body tries to pound some ordinary common sense into him!" sputtered Tildy. She was a proper person and always called the extraordinary old widower for whom she kept house MISTER Adams, though she was the only one who dared to answer him back.

"His bark is worse than his bite," said Mother. "He'll probably be in pretty soon."

"Yes," said Tildy tartly. "All aches and pains and wonderin' why I didn't call him an hour ago! He'll be needin' a nice hot supper to fix him up, I'm thinkin', so I must be gettin' along." With that she swooped up the laundry basket and hurried into the house.

Mother, glancing at her watch, joined Aunt Alice on the porch. They decided it was time to put the finishing touches on a Saturday-night supper of baked beans and brown bread, cold potato salad, and strawberry shortcake. They well knew that the rabbit barbers outside ("Pole and all," said Aunt Alice) would be tired and ravenous now that the barbering was so nearly done.

Uncle Toby, having finished Polar, was clipping Frosting's chubby thighs. He had tucked her head under his left arm and, grasping her tail in his left hand, was cutting away in great style. Daddy had Feather on her back in his lap and was clipping the wool from her round tummy. Sandy was allowed to trim their woolly tails.

"Well, that's that!" said Uncle Toby at last. "Here you are, Mary Jane, eleven or twelve ounces of Angora, and it's all yours!"

Mary Jane looked at the fine, thick wool with its soft sheen in the sunlight. It was heaped in a lustrous pile on the crinkly brown paper, like a strange summer snowdrift. It was irresistible. Her hands flew to it and buried themselves in its downiness. All hers. This was a present worth having! Maybe, it occurred to her for the first time, *maybe* the loom might help make a brighter summer of it after all!

Pondering this, she gathered the wool into a large cooky tin. It was lined with wax paper and had a tightly fitting cover so that the wool would be safely stored till next Wednesday. On that day she and Mother were going to take it over to Miss Merrill's, who knew how to spin.

As for Polar, Feather, and Frosting, they were almost beside themselves with happiness, dancing along the runway with high leaps and double kicks. They looked so much smaller and lighter without their heavy fur that Sandy gave them an extra large supper that evening of parsnips, apple parings, and cauliflower leaves. He grinned as he watched their gay and carefree antics. He knew just how it felt suddenly to be free like that, as each spring the glorious time came when he didn't have to wear his long winter underwear any more.

III

Merry Spinster

MARY JANE scrambled under her father's bed and pulled out his other blue leather slipper. She put the pair of them on the shelf in his closet and hung up his wine-colored bathrobe which had been draped over a bedpost. Honestly, Daddy's as bad as Sandy about putting things away! she thought as she started to make his rumpled bed. No matter how carefully she tucked in the sheets and blankets, the next morning they were always kicked out and tossed in a cluttered heap. So today, because it was Wednesday and she was in such a hurry, she hardly tucked them in at all. She merely gave the bed what Tildy called "a lick and a promise." Luckily, beds were easier to make in the summertime, for most of the bulky blankets were stored away in moth balls. Besides, with the candle-wick spread smoothed over on top, you'd barely notice the ridges of wrinkles underneath.

Mother's bed was scarcely mussed because she moved so little in her sleep. Mary Jane swiftly put it in order. There was still Ditto's crib to do; but, even in spite of her haste, Mary Jane couldn't resist the lure of Mother's shining silver jewelry box which stood on the middle of her mahogany bureau between two tall perfume bottles and some silver-framed baby pictures of the young Mac-Gregors.

Mary Jane, leaning against the bureau, gazed into the mirror above it. She gathered her long hair back behind her ears and viewed them critically. They were nice ears, small and close to her head, with pale pink lobes. Holding her breath, she unclasped the lid of the silver jewelry box and opened it without a sound. It was lined with sea-green velvet. Deeply intent, she searched through a sparkling cluster of beads, chains, brooches, and trinkets until she found the treasure she sought—a pair of old gold-leaf earrings shaped like roses, full blown, with a tiny diamond, glistening like a teardrop, in the center of each. Mary Jane hadn't tried them on for several weeks and had almost forgotten how sweet they looked as they lay there in the palm of her hand.

Delicately, she screwed them on until they pinched a little, first the left and then the right. She held up Mother's hand mirror to admire them, slowly turning her head from side to side with gracious nods and gentle smiles. How elegant they were! And how lovely to be a lady, wearing gold and diamond earrings to teas and parties and dances! She wondered if she'd ever look like those pretty ladies in

Mother's magazines. Surely she had already changed a great deal from that plump-cheeked baby, with large, loose curls, laughing up at her from the silver frame. That had been taken a whole ten years ago. What would she be like ten years from now? She stared hard at her small, serious face, but had to give up because there wasn't a clue. Oh, how she wanted real adventures to happen to herself, to go away wherever in the world she pleased. But real adventures don't happen to people who are eleven and have to stay at home. It took so *long* to grow up—if only the slow-poke time till then would hurry by!

"Beds made, dear?" Mother called from downstairs. She had apparently missed the clatter of Mary Jane's sandals overhead.

Startled, Mary Jane hastily put down the mirror and answered, "All but Ditto's. My goodness, how Daddy tosses up his bed!" as though she had been straightening it out these many minutes.

"When you finish," continued Mother, at the foot of the stairs, "I'd like you to run over and tell Tildy that you and I'll be away this afternoon." Tildy had kindly offered to keep an eye on the two boys whenever Mother and Mary Jane went out together. Sandy was capable enough about answering the telephone and playing with Ditto, but Mother always felt better knowing that Tildy was within easy watching distance.

Mary Jane unscrewed the earrings and carefully laid them away in the jewelry box where she had found them. Then she scurried into the southeast corner bedroom shared by Ditto and Sandy. She liked Ditto's crib even if he didn't. The sheets and blankets were half-size, and the seersucker spread was supposed to be crinkly whether there were blanket wrinkles underneath or not. Mary Jane finished it in jig time, ran a comb through her dangling hair, and dashed downstairs.

Mother was putting a cake tin of creamy white dough

into the hot oven for tonight's dessert. Her face was flushed and warm. "Tell Tildy we'll be back by five," she said as she dusted off her floury hands, "and thank her very much."

"All right," said Mary Jane, running her finger along the rim of the mixing bowl. It tasted good, so she stayed to lick the sticky spoon as well.

"Hurry up, dear!" urged Mother, putting away the calico pot holders and shutting the drawer with a shove.

Mary Jane started out. "Save the frosting pan for us!" she called as she opened the back screen door and accidentally let in a couple of buzzing flies.

The yard seemed idle and deserted. Sandy and Ditto were playing somewhere out in the woods which bordered the back of the MacGregors' lot. The three pinkish rabbits, newly shorn, were sleepily sunning themselves in their pens. Only a faint breeze stirred from the east, ruffling the grass and making the flowers nod in the old-fashioned garden which fringed the well-worn path leading toward Ebenadams' house.

Mary Jane stopped halfway to watch a sparrow take his bath. He hopped in and out of the old tin basin which rested on a discarded chopping block, with a surprised chirp whenever the water splashed his wings. He flew away at once when his bright beady eyes spied Tom,

Ebenadams' black-and-white cat. Tom, haughtily ignoring the silly sparrow, ambled over to nuzzle his nose against Mary Jane's ankles.

"Hello, Tommy, Tom-Tom," said Mary Jane, picking him up in her arms. As she continued along the dirt path she rubbed his head behind the ears until he rumbled his purring thanks.

"Speaks to cats, 'stead o' to people, does she!" commented a gruff voice from within the shingled shed.

Mary Jane jumped and Tom leaped to the ground. She hadn't noticed, as she passed by, that the wide shed door had been flung open on its rusty hinges to let in the morning light. Going back, she paused for a moment on the smoothed step of the threshold, blinking her eyes to get them used to the darkened interior. Soon she could make out the roughly hewn pine-board walls lined with shelves and rows of tools. Bottles of all sizes, jars, and crocks were stored in one dim corner; wooden horses, chests, and boxes in another. The planked floor, nut brown in a slanting patch of sunshine, was sprinkled with curly yellow shavings from newly planed wood. A littered workbench of solid oak stood in front of the one bare window; hovering over it the dark shape of a gaunt old man could be seen.

"Ebenadams!" cried Mary Jane. "Good morning!"

" 'Bout time," he asserted dryly. Like rope, he was lean,

tough, and yellow brown. His prominent, clean-shaven cheekbones were tinged with red, reminder of a fierce winter frostbite, and from beneath shaggy brows, over-hanging deeply caved sockets, keen blue eyes glittered forth. He had a vigorous growth of tousled white hair, surprising for such an old man, and a jutting chin that was square and firm.

"Is the little birdhouse nearly finished?" asked Mary Jane, catching sight of the small, pointed roof he was measuring. Ebenadams' gnarled, blue-veined hands, large knuckled and long fingered, could make or mend any-thing from scarecrows to saltcellars.

"Can't say so," he answered in no particular hurry. "But I reckon nests will do till it is."

Mary Jane stooped down to stroke Dick, the sleek black cat who hunched his back, tail stuck straight in the air. Harryette, the fat yellow-as-wax one, rolled in the shav-ings. Big Tom sprang into Ebenadams' lap, begging to be scratched.

"Scat!" he commanded, shoving the cat to the floor with an angular elbow. Ebenadams was wearing a long-sleeved gray flannel shirt, frayed at the open throat and worn thin from many a brisk and soapy scrubbing—a tribute of Tildy's tireless energy.

"You always push Tommy off," said Mary Jane,

wondering aloud, "and yet he always comes back."

"Beggar for punishment, you mean?" inquired Eben-adams, cocking an eyebrow.

"Oh no!" exclaimed Mary Jane. "But you don't ex-actly spoil him, you know."

"More power to him, then," declared Ebenadams, pounding a nail into the birdhouse roof with the sure, deft aim of his hammer. "To keep a-strivin' fer somethin' that's hard to get is a purty good way to be, seems to me."

"At least he has a chance of getting what he wants," sighed Mary Jane, leaning against the doorjamb.

"Why, child, everybody has a chance of getting what he wants. Because everybody wants the same thing, cats included!" He faced her then, one patient hand out-stretched. "They want to be happy—that's all. Whether they set around wishin' fer the moon with a fence around it or dig ditches to feed their families, there's jest one thing they're doin' it fer—to be happy. There's all kinds o' ways o' tryin'. Some folks find a way that suits 'em and some folks don't. Takes a lot o' time and trouble, mebbe, to settle on the way that's yours, but there's nothin' that kin beat that feelin' once you find it—as I've got a peculiar hunch you'll soon see!"

"Honestly?" asked Mary Jane with intense eagerness. Her cheeks were as pink as Mayflowers. It was so splendid

of Ebenadams, she thought, to tell her how it was with
folks, as though she were already one of them herself. Instead, like most other grownups, he might well have said
to stop fussing—to realize that being young is the happiest
time of your life. And she was tired of hearing that, because she knew that it wasn't so. Yet Ebenadams had also
said he thought she'd soon be finding what she wanted.
"Do you really think so?" she asked.

"Mark my words," predicted Ebenadams, returning to
his work on the little birdhouse. "Now be off with you."

Mary Jane waved good-by. "See you tonight!" she
called. Usually in the evenings, after the supper dishes
were done and Ditto was having his bath, Mary Jane and
Sandy would sit on the rail of Ebenadams' side porch
while he smoked his pipe and rocked in his creaking old
Salem rocker. Together they would watch the darkening
skies, and sometimes—you could never tell just when—
Ebenadams would tell them a wonderful story. . . .

"Morning, Tildy," smiled Mary Jane, pressing her
nose against the back screen door of the roomy kitchen.
Tildy, who "came by the day," showed up at eight o'clock
sharp each morning and left promptly at six each evening.
What the rest of her name was, or where she lived, nobody knew.

"Don't you come in!" cautioned Tildy through the

window. "I've just waxed the linoleum."

"I came up to say that Mother and I are invited over to
Miss Merrill's this afternoon," said Mary Jane. "She's
going to show us how to spin the rabbits' wool into yarn."

"Do tell!" exclaimed Tildy. "There isn't a thing that
mite of a person can't turn her hand to!" For many years
Miss Merrill had been the favorite teacher at Red Oak
Grammar School. Mary Jane and Sandy had both had her
in third grade, and so had Mother when she was a little
girl. Last year Miss Merrill, though still bright as a bird,
had retired from schoolteaching a little regretfully.

"The boys'll be home this afternoon," said Mary Jane.

"I'll keep my weather eye peeled for them, then," said
the faithful Tildy. "Where are they now?"

"Out in the woods, I guess," answered Mary Jane.

Sandy, at that moment, was busily tugging at a torn
piece of tar paper which he had found on top of an aban-
doned henhouse. By pulling it over the interlacing
branched roof of his camp, it made a splendid waterproof
shelter. Finally satisfied with its arrangement, he stood
back to admire the whole effect. In each corner grew a
young maple sapling, forming the framework which sup-
ported the three walls of stout branches, thickly leaved.
The tangled underbrush inside had been cut down and
weeded out, roots and all, leaving a soft earth floor which

Sandy, in his moccasins, leveled by constant stamping and padding. The new roof was a humdinger!

That job done, Sandy loitered along the crooked path to locate Ditto, who had wandered away by himself. Beyond Big Rock and across the narrow brook, down where the maidenhair fern and skunk cabbage grew, he traveled, deeper and deeper into the heart of the woods. He was so light of foot that scarcely a bushy-tailed squirrel scampered out of his way. At last Sandy spotted Ditto. On the sun-dappled ground he was stretched out flat on his stomach under tall pitchy pine trees, deeply engrossed. Beside him was Sandy's black-visored baseball cap filled with a heap of fresh green pine needles.

"Busy?" asked Sandy, leaning against a tree trunk, with his hands in his pockets.

"Mmm," mumbled Ditto, not looking up. He was trying to prick the base of a single pine needle with the rusty point of a common pin.

Sandy watched in silence.

"All needles got eyes but pine needles," said Ditto, starting on another, with the patience of a watchmaker.

Sandy stared at the hundreds of needles in the cap and then glanced up at the thickly clustered trees.

"Figure on putting eyes in all these this morning?" he asked.

"Oh no! There's lots——"

A long, loud whistle chirruped through the woods— one long blow and two short.

"Lunch is ready!" cried Sandy, scooping up the baseball cap and putting it on so that the needles-without-eyes tumbled out in a shower about his head.

"Piggyback!" Ditto called, scrambling after Sandy.

Sandy swung him up on his shoulders and Ditto clutched his ears. "Giddyap!" he shouted hungrily.

For lunch they had big bowls of vegetable soup. Mary Jane ate hers quickly, while she wondered whether or not spinning would be hard to learn. Sandy and Ditto, however, were very slow, counting the peas in their soup, spoonful by spoonful. Sandy counted eighty-four and Ditto sixty-three.

"More, please?" Ditto asked Mother, hoping to catch up to his big brother's record with another bowl.

"You have to begin over again with seconds," said Sandy, who knew the rules.

"Oh," said Ditto, crestfallen. "Guess I'm ready for a 'lasses cooky then, Mummy." After dessert the three of them made short work of the frosting pan.

When the town-hall clock struck three, Ditto was having his nap and Sandy was brushing his rabbits. Mary Jane, carrying the cooky tin of wool, was standing by Mother's side while she turned the knob of Miss Merrill's old-fashioned front doorbell. Her house always reminded Mary Jane of a queen's best hat with a high pink crown and a black lace border. It was a tall brick house surrounded by a fancy wrought-iron fence; it had a gabled roof and many windows. For over eighty years it had been the home of the Merrills, but now Miss Merrill was the only one left. She lived there all alone.

At Mother's ring Miss Merrill, who had been watching through the window for them, promptly opened the door.

"Do come in, my dears!" she said. Though plump as a turnover, she was no taller than Mary Jane. Two silvery curls bobbed at each side of her apple-round face, and a pair of black-rimmed spectacles were perched on her nose. In her green-and-white dress she looked cool and crisp as a lettuce leaf.

Crumpet, her taffy-colored cocker spaniel, bounded into the front parlor at their heels, wagging his tail in welcome. He plopped himself on the hooked rug at Mary Jane's feet.

"I imagine the sooner we start to spin, the better you'll like it," Miss Merrill said at once to Mary Jane.

Mary Jane nodded with a shy smile. She had feared they might spend most of the afternoon on lady-talk. Removing the lid of the cooky tin, she showed Miss Merrill the wool.

"How fluffy it is!" admired Miss Merrill, putting both hands into it to feel its silky texture. "I declare, I've spun the hair of cats and dogs and goats and what not, but this rabbit wool is as nice as any I've ever seen! It's going to make splendid yarn. If you'll excuse me, I'll get my spindle right away."

Mother unfolded her needlepoint and began to stitch while Mary Jane peeped out from the depths of a great wing chair. She had never been in a schoolteacher's house before. Yet nothing, she was surprised to discover, could be more unlike what she had expected to find—there was neither a stack of books on the desk nor an American flag in the corner. Ornate lace curtains hung at the windows, and on the globular lamps were frivolous prisms and painted roses. From the elaborately papered walls portraits of Miss Merrill's ancestors stared down their noses at her in a prim but friendly way.

"Did I keep you waiting long?" asked Miss Merrill, returning with two strange-looking sticks. One she placed on the table at her side, the other she held up for Mother and Mary Jane to see.

"This is a spindle," she explained. "Just a plain wooden disk with a stick stuck through the center—like a candle in a holder. With the yarn I'm making on it now I plan to knit mittens for the Cory children across the street."

"What kind of wool is that?" asked Mary Jane, who could see that it wasn't nearly so fine as the rabbits'.

"Sheep's fleece," answered Miss Merrill, "and it came from my milkman's farm. Look, let me show you how the spindle works."

Miss Merrill laid the fleece along the back of her left hand and deftly fluffed out a few strands with her thumb and forefinger. These strands she joined to the yarn already started on the spindle. With her other hand she twirled the spindle like a top. The twisting strands of fleece were becoming yarn before their very eyes! Miss Merrill spun for them until the spindle, dangling from the long, smooth piece of newly made yarn, reached to the floor.

"Spindle spinning is older than the hills," she said as she wound the long strand of yarn around the stick just above the disk.

"Don't stop yet," begged Mary Jane; so Miss Merrill spun for them again and again. It looked like more fun than Sandy's yo-yo.

"Want to try it?" she asked Mary Jane. "Down, Crumpet!" she scolded as he jumped into Mary Jane's chair when she got up. "Shame on you!" Crumpet apologetically went over to sit by Mother, who gave him a genial pat.

Mary Jane, with the fleece held tightly in her hand, began to spin with the help of Miss Merrill, who got the spindle turning for her. It wasn't easy at first, and she tried to work slowly to get it right. Every so often she fell into the right rhythm. How exciting it was to feel the fleece making a twist and becoming yarn! At last the spindle touched the floor. Mother and Miss Merrill clapped their hands and eagerly looked at her work.

"My yarn's sort of lumpy," admitted Mary Jane. And so it was, fat and thin by turns, as though it had swallowed little pills every now and then. But it was yarn nevertheless, and Mary Jane had spun it herself.

"You keep practicing awhile," Miss Merrill said brightly, "and by the time I have tea ready I'll warrant the spindle will be full."

It very nearly was, too, when Miss Merrill came back bearing a heavily laden tray which she set on the cherry-wood table. Soon they were all sitting around it, Mother and Mary Jane on the sofa and Miss Merrill in a Windsor chair, cheerily pouring tea.

"I always like a cup of tea," Miss Merrill said, passing one to Mother along with a thin silver spoon and hem-stitched napkin. "Even on a very warm day I think it's so invigorating!"

"Oh, so do I!" agreed Mary Jane, to whom a cup of real tea with sugar and milk was a rare treat on any kind of a day. On the pink luster plates were golden popovers, piping hot, and little pats of butter made in acorn molds. There were peach preserves and crispy raisin cookies, as well as wedges of spongecake sprinkled with powdered sugar.

"Here, dear, do have some more cake," Miss Merrill urged Mary Jane, who was feeding tidbits to Crumpet. Miss Merrill and Mother were having a cozy chat, but Mary Jane hardly listened, for her mind kept going back to the spindle. She had a question on the tip of her tongue, and as soon as there was a likely pause in the conversation she asked, "Miss Merrill, what do you do next with the yarn on the spindle?"

"You watch," smiled Miss Merrill, putting down her teacup. She went over to the table and got the other strange-looking stick she had left there.

Because this stick had a crossbar top and bottom, it looked to Mary Jane like a couple of capital "Ts" laid end to end. "Whatever is it for?" she asked.

"It's a reel for winding your yarn properly," said Miss Merrill. "If you'll hold the spindle for me, Mary Jane, I'll wind the yarn from that onto this. It's called a niddy noddy."

So saying, she tied the yarn from the spindle to one end of the niddy noddy, and, holding the stick by the mid-

dle with her left hand, proceeded to loop the yarn from end to end with a brisk bobby motion. In and out, in and out, arranging the yarn in a most orderly way.

"Niddy noddy, niddy noddy,
Two heads with one body!"

Miss Merrill chanted tunefully. The old rhyme delighted Mother and Mary Jane, who chimed in the chorus.

"We must remember that one for Ditto," said Mother. "He'll love it!"

When the niddy noddy held all of the hand-spun yarn from the spindle, Miss Merrill let them examine it. Three of the niddy noddy ends were slightly turned in to keep the yarn from slipping, but the fourth, they noticed, was straight and smooth, so from that one Miss Merrill easily slid the yarn and twisted it into a knot.

"That's all there is to it," she said.

"When may I spin with the rabbits' wool?" Mary Jane asked eagerly.

"I'll start some on this empty spindle for you, if you like," answered Miss Merrill. "You can take it home with you to show Sandy the way you spin. Next time you come over we'll use the spinning wheel up in my work-room. The idea is just the same, only with a spinning wheel it goes along more quickly."

Miss Merrill took some of the rabbits' hair from the cooky tin and put it into a paper bag for Mary Jane to take home with the spindle, so that she would be all set to spin at a moment's notice.

"We can't thank you enough, Miss Merrill," said Mother, shaking Miss Merrill's hand as they prepared to go.

"Nonsense," said Miss Merrill. "Thank the rabbits!"

By the time they left her house it was already after five o'clock. The walk of three blocks was a pleasant one, and the day was cooler now. Coming along Hawthorne Street, they were suddenly aware of peculiar sounds which grew distinctly louder and louder as they ap-proached the MacGregor house. Hurrying at once, Mother and Mary Jane rushed in the front door. In Daddy's den they heard the thundering clatter of hoofbeats and the deafening roar of a bellowing male: "Up and after 'em, comrades!"

"Dynamo again," groaned Mother. At least she was relieved that the noisy din meant nothing more serious. "Turn that radio down, boys!" she cried above the racket. "How you do take advantage when I'm not here to check you!"

Dynamo the Daring, Cowboy Crusader of the Western Wilds, went through his perilous paces every evening, Monday to Friday, from five to five-fifteen. Sandy would almost rather go without his supper than miss one of his thrilling adventures. Lately Ditto, too, was listening as devotedly as his brother. The secret of Dynamo's astounding success was Goodwheat Cereal, and Sandy would eat no other.

"Do you know what?" Mary Jane said blithely to her mother when the radio tale was over and peace restored. "That makes two ways of spinning a yarn in one afternoon! And it's more fun than I thought."

IV

Wheels and Reels

"NO, SANDY, you cannot have another. Two bowlfuls of hot cereal for breakfast in the middle of July are quite enough," said Mother, and rinsed out the pan.

"Gee whiz," Sandy said glumly, "that's not so much."

"By the way," she added, twinkling at his disappointment, "I had to open a new box of Goodwheat this morning."

"Hey, Mother, did you?" he shouted, jumping up and catching her around the waist. "Oh boy, oh boy, oh boy!" He whirled her around the kitchen floor till she panted for breath and laughingly begged him to stop.

Ditto gleefully beat time with his spoon in the air. Daddy put down his coffee cup and looked up from his newspaper to ask, "Mother, what's gotten into our son?"

"That's the *fifteenth* box top!" exclaimed Sandy, beside himself with joy. "Where is it, Mom, where is it?"

he asked, opening the cupboard doors with a clatter and hauling out the contents helter-skelter.

"On the second shelf, dear," answered Mother. She retied her apron strings and helped Mary Jane to clear off the table.

Sandy ripped the lid from the red-and-white cardboard box. A little black arrow, under which was printed "Gold Coin," pointed to a bright solid yellow circle stamped on the center of the box top. With a pair of scissors Sandy jaggedly cut out the circle and held it unbelievingly between his fingers. Here was the fifteenth and last gold coin he needed to fill his Goodwheat Money Bag. On the door of Sandy's closet hung a paper chart which pictured a large bag with fifteen circles in it. Each Goodwheat box top contained one gold coin, to be pasted in a circle on the chart. Because there were at least thirty servings of cereal to a box, it had taken many months to acquire fifteen box tops. Only Sandy ate hot cereal in the summer, so a single box lasted a long while. (Each morning he used to say dismally, "Look at all that's left—I can hardly wait to get hungry again!") Now the end had come and the reward was his. He had but to mail the filled Money Bag Chart to Dynamo the Daring, and Dynamo would send him, Sandy MacGregor, a large Gold Badge of Merit! He was in need of a new badge, too, because the New York World's Fair button that Mr. Whipple had given him was becoming scratched and rusty.

After Sandy, with much love and labor, had composed a letter of thanks to Dynamo on Mother's best blue stationery, he folded the Money Bag Chart with great care and placed it inside the envelope. He fervently hoped it wouldn't be lost in the mail. In fact, he decided he'd better take it right down to the Post Office himself to make sure.

"Leaving now?" he asked Mary Jane. She was going over to Miss Merrill's to spin. Her spindle was plumply wound with rabbit yarn which she had spun at home. Sandy thought spindle spinning was great fun and had even made a spindle for himself, which he painted a dashing red. They had daily contests to see whose yarn would reach the floor more quickly.

Sandy walked as far as Miss Merrill's house with Mary Jane. His letter to Dynamo was safely stored in his trouser pocket. As they arrived, Miss Merrill was in her garden, weeding pink and purple phlox.

"Hello there!" she called, delighted to see them so early in the day. Sandy and Crumpet had a spirited tussle on the lawn, and if Miss Merrill hadn't been so speedy about shutting the gate, Crumpet would have tagged gladly after Sandy as he continued on his way to the Post Office.

Miss Merrill took off her garden gloves and put away her trowel.

"Bless me, but I'm glad Sandy went in for raising rabbits," she said. "He might have chosen goldfish or canaries."

"Or polliwogs," laughed Mary Jane. "He used to bring those home by the dozen. I guess rabbits really are the best."

"And you'll think so even more after you spin their wool on the spinning wheel," promised Miss Merrill as she buttoned on her smock. "Shall we go up now?"

They climbed the stairs to the sunny, cluttered workroom. Though it was large and square, there was hardly space to turn around. Never before had Mary Jane beheld such a curious jumble of looms and frames and reels.

She was quite taken by the little painted chests and the desk that had so many cubbyholes. But nicest of all were the enormous spinning wheel which filled one corner and the small black one, on three plump legs, which stood before an open window. The white curtains were drawn back, and a pot of geraniums rested on the sill. Sparrows were chirping on a telegraph wire outside.

"I like this room," said Mary Jane.

"Thank you, dear," said Miss Merrill. "I like it too. It's a jolly sort of a room."

"And yet it's filled with work to do!" Mary Jane said softly, with wonder in her eyes. She thought more kindly of the little loom in her own room at home.

"Sounds like some sort of a secret, doesn't it?" smiled Miss Merrill. "Come, let me show you the wheel."

She set aside the willow basket of colored spools which was on the seat of a Hitchcock chair and sat down in front of the small spinning wheel. It was already threaded with the driving band, a long, continuous piece of twine that went twice around the wheel, a strand in each groove, and once around the bobbin.

"These two uprights are called the Maidens," Miss Merrill said to Mary Jane, who stood by her side, "and the horizontal bar between them, which holds the bobbin, is called the Mother of All. See how the Maidens and the

Mother of All move toward the wheel when I turn this handle? The Mother of All, you see, has to be screwed near the wheel before you begin."

She turned the handle and got ready to spin the snowy rabbits' wool. She joined its fluffed-out strands to a piece of yarn already attached to the wheel.

"Here we go!" announced Miss Merrill. She pressed her foot on the treadle, and immediately the wheel whirled around. The fluffed-out strands of wool were at once twisted into yarn and drawn in, winding themselves like magic onto the bobbin. The soft whir-whir of the little wheel hummed as it spun, as contented a sound as big Tom's purring.

"Your hands do all the work when you spin with a spindle," said Miss Merrill, never stopping. "This way, your foot helps out. Thanks to the treadle, it twists and winds the yarn for you, leaving both hands free to pull the wool."

For several mornings Mary Jane came over to Miss Merrill's to practice turning the wheel with her foot. She treadled until its rhythm became so much a part of her that she could carry on a lively conversation with Miss Merrill and not miss a single beat.

Miss Merrill would sit near by, busily hooking her rug of remnants from the textile mills. Often she'd tell Mary

Jane about spinning long ago. "In colonial times," she said, "all young girls had wedding chests, and they took great pride in filling them with beautiful linens and coverlets which they made themselves. Each one, whether she was rich or poor, knew how to spin. Indeed, regular spinning matches were held outdoors in the town commons. And a minister preached sermons to them while they worked!"

As for the great wheel in the corner, Miss Merrill said that it had been in her family for over one hundred years. She seldom used it any more, because spinning wheels, unless frequently oiled and in good repair, were "pernickety things." Besides, she really didn't have enough room. Ladies in those days spun in their spacious attics or on the wide barn floors. They were graceful persons, supple and lithe, because spinning was an art of such dignity and poise. The spinster, after giving the great wheel a quick turn, would step alertly backward for a few steps with the twisting yarn held high in her left hand above her head. Then, coming swiftly forward, she would let the yarn wind around the bobbin. Backward and forward she danced to the murmuring wheel—sometimes she stepped twenty miles in a single day!

In less than a week Mary Jane was really spinning. The bobbin gradually filled with row upon row of lovely white yarn, bright as stars. Mary Jane never grew tired of watching it thicken.

"Do you always use a niddy noddy for winding the yarn?" she asked as it mounted higher and higher.

"Oh no!" Miss Merrill said in surprise. "Haven't you heard the clock reel talk yet? Deary me, how could I have forgotten that!" From behind one of the large looms she dragged out a wooden reel to the middle of the room. At the top of its tall, narrow stand was a large rimless wheel with six spokes. Each spoke had a small crossbar, and at the hub of the wheel was a handle.

"Turn the handle till it tells you to stop," Miss Merrill prompted mysteriously as she attached some green yarn to one of the crossbars. "I'm not going to say a single word!"

Mary Jane timidly grasped the handle and turned. The wheel went round at once, winding yarn on the crossbars as it went. She turned slowly at first, then faster and faster. She turned and turned, but nothing happened except for the mounting rows of yarn. She turned it eighty times. Suddenly a snapping "CRACK!" burst forth. Mary Jane let go of the handle and drew back in astonishment.

"There!" laughed Miss Merrill. "The clock reel has now wound enough yarn and is telling you so! You then tie the circle of yarn and take it off the reel. When you have four circles of yarn like this you will have, in all, one skein."

Mary Jane couldn't go back to her spinning until she had made the clock reel talk "just once more, please!" "CRACK!" it reported after eighty turns. Mary Jane was charmed. She hoped it wouldn't be long before the rabbits' wool, all white and finely spun, could be wound in skeins on the talking reel.

When she got home that evening she told her family all about it at the supper table. Mother and Daddy and Ditto were very interested and asked her many questions. She was so busy answering them, using both hands to describe the reel, that she didn't notice how sullen and silent Sandy was. He hardly touched his baked potato, bolted his tapioca pudding, and then begged to be excused. He didn't wait to dry the dishes, as usual, but immediately hurried out of the house. Sandy was in trouble.

During the afternoon Sandy's rabbits had been so full of fun that he had done a rare thing: he let them out of their pens and played with them on the grass. Ditto was so overjoyed he turned a couple of somersaults. Feather and Frosting capered around the sunflower stalks like two frilly little ballet dancers, and Polar leaped through Sandy's arms every time he held them like a hoop. After their frolic, Sandy and Ditto fed the rabbits peas and cabbage and turnip roots and sent them off to bed, safely locked in their cozy hutch.

Ditto had then scurried into the house to show Mother the three-cornered tear he had just gotten in the knee of his overalls. Sandy, left alone, washed out the rabbits' dishes with the garden hose and carried them, still dripping, to the garage. As he stacked them on the shelf he noticed his black-visored baseball cap lying in the middle of the cement floor where Ditto must have dropped it earlier in the day. Sandy picked it up and tossed it high into the air. He tried to catch the cap on his head—and just missed. It fell against his ear and tumbled to the floor. Sandy tried again, this time hurling it even higher. To his extreme disgust, the cap got caught on a narrow beam which ran along the eaves. He grabbed a handy rake and tried to pry it loose. But the rake didn't quite reach.

"Supper's ready, Sandy!" Mary Jane called.

"Just a minute!" he shouted, his eyes darting about the garage for something suitable on which he could stand. They lighted on Mother's antique footstool. The very thing! By turning it up on end it gave him even greater height. Gingerly he mounted the rocking rose-carved

footstool, both hands balancing the long-handled rake. With one energetic lunge he dislodged the cap and wrenched it free so forcefully that the footstool suddenly gave way and he lost his balance. Down came Sandy, cap, rake, and all, with a resounding crash!

"Supper, Sandy!" Mary Jane called impatiently.

"Coming!" he croaked, half dazed by his fall and terrified at the thought of the shattered footstool. Though somewhat bumped and bruised, he was not hurt. With a sinking feeling he crawled over to the footstool to examine the damage he had done. At the sight of it Sandy's heart did a tailspin.

One leg was entirely broken off, its ragged edge in pitiful splinters; the finish in several places was badly scratched and battered. He realized at once that here was a repair job far too big for him to tackle alone. He had to have help. Hurriedly Sandy gathered up the pieces and put them, for the time being, in Ditto's cart. What to do next he didn't know, except that he had to decide on a remedy right away. Worried and absorbed in thought, he headed toward the house. His black-visored baseball cap lay forgotten on the cement floor in the garage.

Luckily, during supper Mary Jane was so wrapped up in wheels and reels and things that nobody paid any attention to him. At last the meal was over and he was free to get back to the garage. He had put one plan in mind—one hope only.

By lugging the footstool furtively behind the hydrangea hedges, he escaped his family's notice and made his way, roundabout and difficult, to Ebenadams' house. Silently he crept along the back porch, his heart hammering wildly against his ribs. Through the screen door he could see the old man having a sober game of solitaire on the kitchen table. Tildy had gone. A lone cricket chirruped in the grass, and the evening shadows deepened.

"Come in, boy!" called the strong voice of Ebenadams, who had not stirred in his chair. "Don't gape there like a gargoyle on a tombstone!"

It was too late to run away. Sandy had to face Ebenadams with the broken footstool. Hesitantly he shifted his burden under one arm, opened the door, and, in miserable silence, stood at Ebenadams' elbow.

Ebenadams continued his solitaire with great deliberation, laying down the cards one by one. The room was growing steadily darker. Sandy gulped nervously as the last card was slapped to the table. The horsehair upholstery of the footstool made his tired arm burn and itch, but he did not dare to scratch it.

"Well?" asked Ebenadams, turning in his chair and looking up at Sandy's face. If he noticed the footstool he made no mention of it, but waited silently.

Thus encouraged, Sandy stammered out his story. He told it briefly and honestly. He offered no excuses.

"So what are you fixin' to do about it?" asked Ebenadams, squinting his shaggy brows and cocking a sharp eye at Sandy.

"I—I thought maybe you'd mend it for me, please," Sandy faltered from between dry lips. "I could hoe your potato patch like sixty!" he rattled on eagerly, waving the footstool leg in his excitement. "Honest I could. I hoe just dandy. Uncle Toby said so. Or I could mow your grass or pick bushels 'n' bushels of apples, soon as they're ripe, or——"

"Hold on, boy!" interrupted Ebenadams with a quieting gesture. "And, for mercy's sake, set down."

Dejectedly Sandy flopped on the hard kitchen chair. Because both hands still clutched the footstool, he tried unsuccessfully to brush back the damp hair on his forehead with a despondent twist of his elbow. He felt hot and discouraged.

Slowly Ebenadams made his way to the center of the kitchen, fumbled for the dangling light pull, and switched on the light.

"Now let's take a look at this," he said, removing the footstool from Sandy's unresisting arms. He set it up on the kitchen table and examined it closely.

Sandy turned his head to the wall and watched a fly rub its little front legs together as though it knew a splendid joke. Lucky fly!

"Tell you what," said Ebenadams at last. "I'll make a proposition with you, Sandy MacGregor."

Sandy brightened hopefully. He was ready to agree to anything.

"Ferget about hoein' my patch and pickin' my apples—that's got nothin' to do with this." Meditatively Ebenadams turned the broken footstool leg, with its deep carving, in his long-fingered hands. "I'll repair the footstool good as it was afore it got—uh—dislocated. If I do that, I expect you to refinish it—and do a top-notch job to boot! I'll show you how, and I'm warnin' you 'twon't be easy. All this hardened old varnish has got to come off before the wood can be oiled and polished, and there's a mighty lot of pesky little crevices in the carvin' of them roses. It'll take elbow grease, son, and plenty of it. What do you say?"

"Sure I'll do it—sure I will!" Sandy agreed breathlessly, pounding his fists on the table. He was positively glowing with relief. One last worried frown flickered for a moment across his brow. "You won't tell—you won't tell till it's all done?" he asked anxiously.

Ebenadams stood up and held out his hand as a solemn pledge. Sandy wrung it gratefully. "Thanks!" he said

hoarsely. "Gee, Ebenadams, thanks a whale of a lot!" So saying, he rushed out the door.

The air felt cool and good, and the night seemed kindly to him as he sped down the path, happily empty-handed. But, even so, things were different now that he had a dark secret in his heart. He felt the full, fearful weight of it when he arrived home and saw his mother sitting by the radio in the den with Daddy. She was at work on the needlepoint for her footstool. Her nimble fingers seemed to fly. Sandy earnestly hoped she wouldn't be finished too soon.

V

Indian Pudding Party

EBENADAMS came out of the house one evening late in July carrying an old cigar box. Mary Jane and Sandy, who who had been waiting for him, slid off the porch railing and stood each side of the Salem rocker as Ebenadams hitched up his trouser legs and sat down. The sunset was a fiery one, and in its ruddy light they stared curiously at the opened box in his lap. It was filled with Indian arrowheads.

Ebenadams held one of the shapely stone relics in his wrinkled hand. "I recollect I must-a been twelve years old, if I was a day, when I first come across this one," he told them. "Should-a been in school, but it was April—warm and thawin' to beat the band. Touch o' spring fever struck me, I guess, for 'stead-a mindin' my ps and qs in the schoolhouse, I was prowlin' around barefoot on the pebbly banks o' the river, spry as a grasshopper. Used to be an Indian village thereabouts called Amoskeag, which is Indian-talk for Fishin' Place; and that river they fished in, the Indians named Merrimack—Swift Water."

"They were hunters, too, weren't they, Ebenadams?" asked Sandy. "They caught bears in traps and shot birds with bows and arrows!" His eyes were sparkling; he loved to play Indians in the woods.

"Yep, that's how they got their vittles," said Ebenadams, "and many of their tools and weapons made o' bone and shell and flint are good to this day, same as these. They had to make everything for themselves—why, say, Mary Jane, they even had the first kind of a loom!"

"Did they really?" she asked. It never occurred to her, now that she was eleven, that she still could play Indians. "What did it look like?" To Mary Jane the subject of looms had lately become vastly interesting.

"Are you up to the weavin' part yet?" countered Ebenadams. Harryette's gleaming topaz eyes appeared from the leafy shadows.

"Almost," answered Mary Jane, sitting on the rail again with Harryette curled in her lap. "Yesterday Miss Merrill made the warp on her warping board."

"What does that mean?" questioned Sandy. After all, his rabbits started this commotion in the first place, and he felt he had a right to know.

"Well," Mary Jane said slowly, in order to get it right, "the warp means the straight threads that run up and down, and they're held taut on the loom while you weave. But before you put the warp on the loom you have to make it first. You do that on a warping board, which is flat and thick and has seven fat pegs on top. The pegs are stuck around the edge like a fence. Miss Merrill crossed a piece of yarn around them, back and forth, sixty times —making one hundred and twenty threads."

"How did she keep track of so many?" asked Sandy, slapping a pesky mosquito.

"As soon as she had ten white threads of yarn on the pegs, she'd tie them with a little piece of red string."

"Did she use the rabbits' yarn?" he questioned.

"Not yet," said Mary Jane. "The warp's going to be made of silk and wool."

"And then what did she do?"

"You sound like Ditto!" said Mary Jane. "Let's see, she took the warp off the board with the cross sticks. They're a couple of round sticks a little longer than the width of what you're going to weave. When Miss Merrill got through with them, you should have seen those sticks! They were woven right into all those threads, separating each from the other as neat as could be. There were twelve threads to an inch, so whatever I weave'll be ten inches wide. Now the warp's all ready to go on the loom, and by the time it is, my spinning will be done!"

"So you'll weave the weft of hand-spun rabbit yarn into the warp of silk and wool; to make a—what?" asked Ebenadams.

"A web!" Mary Jane answered quickly. "Whatever you weave, it's a web!"

"Even on an Indian loom?" Sandy asked doubtfully.

"Even on an Indian loom," insisted Ebenadams.

"You didn't tell us what one looked like," Mary Jane reminded him. It amazed her that Ebenadams should know about weaving.

"'Twas a simple thing," he said. "The Indians stretched the warp threads 'twixt two poles, which they hung on the limb of a tree. Weight of the lower pole held the threads taut. Wove the weft thread in and out by hand, they did, and beat the web with a flat stick to push the threads together good and tight."

"I wish we were Indians," declared Sandy, aiming an imaginary bow and arrow at a bright star. "Wish we lived in a wigwam by the river, 'stead of a house, and always ate outdoors around a fire. You'd be a good squaw, Mary Jane, 'cause you can spin and almost weave. And Ditto'd be such a funny papoose!"

The next morning Sandy went out to feed the rabbits

with a feather in his hair. He called the rabbits baby buf-
faloes and scanned the horizon for signs of an enemy
smoke signal. Ditto was perplexed.

"Me heap big redskin," grunted Sandy.

"You are not," giggled Ditto, unimpressed. "You're a
red-hair!"

"He's practically a red-*hare!*" punned Mary Jane.

"All right, all right, then," said Sandy, scornful of their

teasing. "Call me Red Wing! . . . CHIEF Red Wing!"

"And I'll be your squaw, Morning Star!" said Mary Jane, nibbling Sandy's irresistible bait in earnest.

"Who am I? Who am I?" clamored Ditto, who had to be a redskin too.

"Let's see, who can Ditto be?" said Mary Jane.

They sat on the grass and considered.

"I have it!" exclaimed Sandy, snapping his fingers. "This morning before you came out, Mary Jane, Ditto said, 'Hi, Niddy Noddy!' to Tildy——"

"What did she say?" Mary Jane asked half fearfully.

"She shook out her mop real hard and said, 'Don't you Niddy Noddy me, young man!' So Ditto can just be Niddy Noddy himself! Niddy Noddy, our Indian papoose!"

Chief Red Wing's first duty was to procure feathers for Morning Star and Niddy Noddy.

"Me go shootum eagle!" he thundered, and sped into the house. In a moment he returned, triumphantly bearing two black-and-white feathers. Morning Star and Niddy Noddy accepted them with low bows to such a mighty hunter. Nobody thought the feathers looked the least bit like those on Mother's old black hat.

From then on they were Indians, all that week and the next one too. From morning till night they wore their

black-and-white feathers, and Mother braided Mary
Jane's hair into two blond pigtails. The following
Wednesday would be Niddy Noddy's fourth birthday.
To celebrate with a party-in-the-house would never do,
they told their parents. They had to have a regular pow-
wow for their papoose!

And so they did. At five o'clock on Wednesday, as
soon as Daddy got home from work, the whole Mac-
Gregor family trooped out to the back yard by the border of the woods. They wore old slacks and sweaters and
skirts. It was a cool evening, with a pleasant breeze blow-
ing. Mary Jane and Mother, each grasping a handle,
lugged between them an enormous picnic basket of food
covered with a linen napkin. Daddy toted two dozen un-
husked ears of Golden Bantam corn, the first of the sea-
son, freshly picked and sent by Uncle Toby especially for
the occasion. Sandy followed in the rear with a wobbling
wheelbarrow of presents. Ditto rode gloriously on top.
He waved excitedly to Ebenadams, who was coming
down the path to join them, bearing a strange-looking
banner. It was the little birdhouse perched on a tall, thin
pole!

In the clearing, where Sandy had piled logs of ash and
elm for kindling and tinder of dried twigs, Daddy struck
a match, and soon the fire was crackling with a merry

blaze. Ebenadams presented the birdhouse to Ditto, who immediately wanted him to "plant" it on the spot.

"Tomorrow morning!" Ebenadams promised him with a chuckle. "Right now we got to rustle up some supper." Together they husked the corn and wrapped the full yellow ears in wet leaves to roast in the hot ashes beside the brown-jacketed sweet potatoes. While the food was roasting, Ebenadams gave each one a handsome pheasant feather to wear, and Ditto opened his presents with fast-flying fingers.

The plump little bundle tied with twine, which came from Cousins Don and Doug, was unwrapped first. It was a fragrant balsam pillow with a green tree stamped on it and the words "Souvenir of the White Mountains—Come Again." In the big white package tied with blue ribbons was a colored picture book of wild animals, and pressed between the pages, for luck, was a four-leaf clover which Mary Jane had found one day in the grass. Sandy's box contained a pair of bright red elastic suspenders. Ditto had to try them on then and there, even though his short brown pants were securely buttoned to his shirt. Tildy had sent a tin of homemade gingersnaps, wafer thin, and Miss Merrill had sent a very old gray-blue pottery plate with the alphabet around the rim in dark blue letters.

Ditto studied the plate thoughtfully. "I can't read what

it says," he admitted, "but I like it very much—I could use it right now!" He sniffed the smoky, food-scented air, and his mouth watered at the sight of the open picnic basket.

They all sat down cross-legged around the leaping fire and reveled in their heaped-up plates. Besides the roasted corn and sweet potatoes there were large, moist, dark and light slices of cold turkey ("A wild one shot by Chief Red Wing!" Daddy grinned), hot buttered bran muffins with pools of fresh honey, and cold milk to drink from green and yellow gourds. For dessert Mother brought on the steaming Indian pudding, a rich gold-brown mixture of molasses and corn meal just out of the oven, with huge scoops of vanilla ice cream melting in thick rivulets on top. They ate till they could hardly swallow another bite.

"It was perfect!" breathed Mary Jane in the gathering darkness.

"Except that without a cake and candles, Ditto can't make a wish," said Sandy.

"Oh, but he can!" Daddy answered, much to their surprise. From the bottom of the big basket he drew out the turkey wishbone, which Mother had saved and dried.

"Hurray!" shouted Ditto. "Come on, Sandy!"

They stood up, and each curled his little finger around a branch of the wishbone, silently making a wish under the stars. Sandy gave Mother's footstool a quick thought and his wish was made. Ditto, although truly fond of his brand-new presents, remembered his crib with a sigh. He, too, had a wish on the tip of his tongue.

"All set?"

"All set!"

"One for a penny, two for a show, three to get ready, and four to—GO!"

They tugged at the bone till it snapped in two.

"I won!" cried Ditto. "Oh, I won on my birthday!" He jumped up and down, barely missing a plate which Mother hastily rescued. She and Daddy picked up the scattered remains of their feast and took them into the house.

Morning Star and Niddy Noddy sat with Ebenadams, watching the dancing red and yellow flames of the fire, which seemed to grow brighter and brighter as the night darkened; while Chief Red Wing, squatting on his heels, toasted marshmallows on a long stick.

"Tell us a story!" said Mary Jane.

"An Indian one!" begged Ditto.

"Tell us about Joe English!" Sandy said eagerly.

"Why, sakes alive, you've heard it forty times or more!" objected Ebenadams, pressing tobacco into the bowl of his pipe—sure sign of a story to come!

"Ditto hasn't heard it, have you, Ditto?" asked Sandy.
"Tell us about Joe English—pleeese."

Ebenadams lit his pipe with a wooden match scratched
on the sole of his high shoe. He puffed a few times and
absently stared at the smoke.

"Once there was an Indian," he began, "who had a
good head on his shoulders, and, what's more, a brave
heart. Lived out New Boston way, he did, where there's
a hill that tops all others. Slopes down nice and easy-like
on one side, but the other—why, it's nothin' but a solid
mass of sheer rock that drops into space! Now this here

Indian, same as his mighty chiefs afore him, was partial to the white folk and called them friends—oh, we was lucky to have a friend like that in them days! It made some other Indians hoppin' mad, though, and sore as hornets. They jeered at him and called him old Joe English, and finally they decided to kill him. . . .

" 'Twas dusk. Joe had been huntin' by hisself in the forest all afternoon and he was plumb wore out. It didn't make him feel no better, neither, to see that band o' hostile Indians sneakin' up on him ready to attack. So what did he do? He run for all he was worth, as fast as his heels could carry him, to give 'em the slip. He was doin' fine, too, when all of a sudden three of the biggest, fastest, meanest Indians o' the lot almost caught up with him! Joe took one look at them and used his head as well as his feet. He changed his course o' direction and made a beeline for the highest hill, speedin' like a streak o' greased lightnin'. The three Indians fell behind, but they kept on comin' all the same. Joe ran like he never run before. When he reached the summit he stopped short in his tracks at the very brink o' that rock-bound precipice and flung hisself behind a clump o' bushes. He held his breath and waited. In a moment the Indians were almost there. Joe's blood ran cold when he felt the ground beneath him shake with the poundin' o' their rushin' feet. But they

was travelin' so fast *they rushed right over the edge!*
Them Indians had hurled theirselves over that cliff afore
you could say 'Jack Robinson!' And Joe English was
saved."

The young MacGregors, their faces bright in the flick-
ering firelight, sighed with relief and thanked him heart-
ily.

"Is it a really-truly story?" asked Ditto, stirring closer
to the waning fire.

"I tell the tale like it was told to me," answered Ebenadams. "But that hill is called Joe English Hill to this very
day, and that's a fact."

"Bedtime for Niddy Noddy!" sang out Daddy as he
and Mother came back at last.

Ditto, trying hard to keep his eyes open, snapped his
new red suspenders with sleepy pride and collected his
balsam pillow, the gingersnaps, and the animal picture
book. He wanted to pick up the birdhouse too, but
Mother told him it might be better to leave it outdoors
where it belonged.

Daddy hoisted Ditto, presents and all, onto his shoulder
and secretly beckoned the others to follow. Wonder-
ingly they filed into the house in back of him as he led the
way upstairs. The lights were on in Ditto's and Sandy's
room. Daddy stood in the doorway and didn't say a word.

Mother and Mary Jane and Sandy and Ebenadams clustered together as quietly as they could, peering in so as not to miss a single move.

Ditto, whose head was nodding heavily, became aware of the unusual stillness and was puzzled. He looked up and blinked his eyes. His mouth made a little round "o." "A bed!" he whispered. It dawned on him that his wishbone wish had come true.

"A *real* bed!" he shouted joyously, wide awake. He clapped his hands and, without even knowing it, dropped the animal book and tin of gingersnaps. "A bed to go with my pillow! Oh, *thank* you!" He gave Daddy a bear hug and wiggled out of his arms.

His old crib was nowhere to be seen. Daddy and Mother must have been dismantling it while Ebenadams had been telling the story. Ditto walked over to his new bed and took in every detail. It was a maple four-poster, side by side and twin to Sandy's own. The clean sheets and coverlet were turned back invitingly.

Ditto threw a kiss to the crowd in the doorway. "Good night!" he said cheerily, and took off his red suspenders.

They answered with a jolly chorus of "Happy Birthday!" and bid him "Good night and sweet dreams!" as they departed. Mother stayed to tuck him in—a blissful papoose in striped pajamas.

VI

Whistlin' Amy Adams

MARY JANE could hardly keep from crying. Tears welled in her eyes and there was a lump in her throat. It was a sultry day not long after Ditto's birthday, so hot that even to move cost considerable effort, and everyone was out of sorts.

Stretched out on her wrinkled bedspread, chin cupped in her hands and propped on her elbows, Mary Jane stared at her little honey-colored loom by the window. The shades were drawn in a futile attempt to keep out the blistering heat and sunlight. The silk-and-wool warp was on the loom, and the flat wooden shuttle was wound with white Angora yarn, hand-spun. All was in readiness at long last—the actual moment of weaving was at hand. But it was beyond Mary Jane's power to begin; she was helpless and confused.

Suddenly she couldn't stand the sight of it a moment longer. Her hair felt heavy and her scalp prickled with warmth. Biting her lower lip to stifle a sob, she got up and left the room, tiptoeing downstairs in her bare feet. Mother was on the davenport in the living room, restlessly trying to sleep away a sick headache. Mary Jane slipped past her and went out the back door into the harsh, bright light of early afternoon. She looked neither to left nor right, but, half running, went directly to the woods.

There it was dim and churchlike, with deep shadows and soft, rustling sounds. She hastened to her "secret place" and cried aloud when she reached it. Away from the main path and hidden by the trees was a small grassy plot by the brook, no larger than one small person. Mary Jane had made angel wings there in last winter's snow: there was just enough room for that. Now it was sweet with ferns and violet leaves, and a few pale bluets.

Mary Jane wept with abandon, her cheek pressed hard

against the damp, mossy ground and her hand splashing in the running water of the shallow brook. It felt good to cry like that. Gradually her narrow shoulders stopped heaving; her tears subsided and she lay very still. They became cool and calm and quiet—she and her secret place.

Thoughts filtered through her mind again, and she re-membered how pleased and happy she had been when she and Miss Merrill completed the beaming of her loom to-gether—could that have been only yesterday! Her spin-ning had long since been finished and the yarn wound on the talking clock reel into great feathery white skeins. Yesterday morning at nine o'clock Miss Merrill had come over to the MacGregors' house to put the silk-and-wool warp on Mary Jane's loom. To Mary Jane the loom was now the most important thing in her room.

"I can't wait to see how it's going to look," she said, following in Miss Merrill's tracks as she set about her task. "Please, may I help?"

"Yes indeed, dear; soon as I get these cross sticks tied to the front beam and the threads spread out. My, but this little loom is a pleasure to work on—you'll be in clover once you're weaving!"

Miss Merrill trotted back and forth, measuring with her yellow tape measure, tightening catches and counting dents in the comblike beater in such a capable sort of way that Mary Jane was more anxious than ever to be useful.

Willingly she took the long hook Miss Merrill gave her and did just as she was told, catching the loops of yarn and sliding them onto the back rod; she got out Mother's sewing scissors and then watched Miss Merrill cut the front loops with quick little snips; and she even did her share in the threading-up. The morning slipped by so quickly they barely noticed the heat.

"There now, that's all done!" pronounced Miss Merrill, highly gratified, after she tested the tension. "And mighty well it looks at that!"

"Oh yes!" agreed Mary Jane, fingering it with delight. The loom now looked a hundred times more intriguing than when Mother had first brought it home.

"There's only the winding of the shuttle with your rabbits' yarn left to do," said Miss Merrill.

It was already lunch time when they finished, but Mary Jane would have gladly gone without hers, so eager was she to weave on her loom right away. Her fingers fairly itched to begin.

"But, my dear, you don't want to start with this!" declared Miss Merrill. "You should practice a bit first."

Mary Jane was dumbfounded. Was it possible that after so many weeks of patience and preparation she *actually* had to wait longer?

Noting her surprise, Miss Merrill said encouragingly, "You can practice as much as you please on one of my looms—just till you get your weaving down pat, that is. Why, it won't take you any time! Then you can make something really worth while on your own loom from the very start."

Mary Jane didn't answer. She wasn't interested in making anything "worth while"—she only wanted to weave on her own loom. Who wouldn't, after spinning those miles and miles of yarn for that very purpose? If Miss Merrill hadn't wanted her to, why didn't she say so before? Forever practicing was a tiresome, senseless idea, and she wanted no more of it. Scalding tears burned in her eyes when, to make matters worse, good, kind Mother sided with Miss Merrill. They both tried to explain to her the importance of practicing—what a shame it would be to waste that lovely yarn on beginner's mistakes, and what difference did just a few more days make, anyhow?—but they didn't understand. Mary Jane felt cheated. She was sick with disappointment.

Finally Mother said to Miss Merrill before she left, "When Mary Jane decides she's ready to practice weaving she'll come over to your house, if you'll be kind enough to have her. Apparently she isn't ready yet." From then on, yesterday and today, the subject had been closed. Mother left it squarely up to Mary Jane.

Mary Jane rolled over on her back with a last sniffle and sighed wearily, staring at the patch of sky overhead. It was a clear, clean blue, with a curving scrap of cloud as starchy white as the collar of Tildy's house dress. Tildy! Tildy would know; Tildy would care! She made up her mind to tell Tildy as soon as possible.

Cheered by her decision, Mary Jane waded in the brook, wiggling the toes of her dusty feet on smooth, embedded stones, the water swirling in silvery loops around her ankles. She bent over and dashed a spray of the cold water on her tearstained cheeks and weepy eyes. She slicked back her tumbled hair with her wet hands, and the trickles of water felt like slim fingers playing on her forehead. Then she straightened her gingham dress and hoped it didn't look too disorderly. Thus refreshed, she called on Tildy with a sprig of checkerberries, which she had picked along the way, in her hand.

Tildy was ironing.

"Of all things to be doing on such a hot day!" Mary Jane exclaimed at the sight of Tildy's perspiring face.

"Wednesday's always been ironin' day in this house, and I'm not one to change it!" declared Tildy grimly. She wet her finger and flicked it on the iron. It sizzled satisfactorily and she put it on the stand.

Mary Jane sat down on the edge of a kitchen chair, careful not to muss the freshly ironed shirt hanging on the back. She didn't know where to begin. "These are for you," she said respectfully, laying her woodsy offering on the thickly padded ironing board. Tildy didn't say anything, but she was touched nonetheless. They ate the round red checkerberries in companionable silence.

"Ain't seen hide nor hair o' you lately," said Tildy, resuming her work. "Been busy?"

Yes, she had been busy, good and busy, and all for nothing, too; that was just it, answered Mary Jane, and poured out her woeful story to Tildy's sympathetic ears. She talked more and more quickly as the complications grew, and was almost breathless with agitation by the time she finished. Didn't Tildy agree that it was mean and unfair of Mother and Miss Merrill to keep her waiting? After all, it hadn't been *her* idea to weave in the first place.

Tildy continued to iron with broad, sweeping strokes. "Depends," she said cryptically.

"On what?" asked Mary Jane, exasperated. "I don't see why I can't weave on my own loom if I want to."

"What's the finished product you got in mind?" probed Tildy.

"Nothing," replied Mary Jane, shaking her head. "I just want to weave on my loom." It was as simple as that.

"If you're makin' nothin', how'll you know when it's done?" Tildy asked innocently.

"I don't know," admitted Mary Jane.

"Suppose in the middle o' nothin' you suddenly took a notion to make *some*thin'—what then?"

"I'd have to start over, I guess."

"And unravel all o' nothin'—what a shame!" lamented Tildy. "Sure would take a heap o' time, too. You couldn't get started on somethin' till you got nothin' all undid."

Mary Jane shifted uneasily. It was a knotty problem and difficult to untangle. She and Tildy had to concentrate very hard. Trying to find a suitable solution was quite a task.

"I have it!" triumphed Tildy, setting down her iron with a clash. "What you need is *two* looms! You could make nothin' on one and somethin' on the other!"

"Why, of course!" Mary Jane brightened. Then she added glumly, "But, Tildy, I have only one loom."

"Wish I had one," said Tildy. "If I did, I'd lend you mine, you can bet on that."

"I—I could use Miss Merrill's—she said so!" suggested Mary Jane.

"Well, why not!" exclaimed Tildy. "You can make nothin' on yours, just like you want, and, when the notion hits you, make somethin' on hers!"

"Or the other way around," Mary Jane planned quickly. "It'd be more fun to make nothing on hers and something on mine with the yarn I've spun myself!"

"So 'twould! That's a prime idea, Mary Jane," approved Tildy. Her head was bent over her work. "When are you aimin' to start?" she inquired offhand.

"I could start tomorrow morning, I guess—yes, Tildy, that's exactly what I'll do!"

"And in the meantime we'll be cogitatin' on what the somethin's goin' to be. How's that?"

"Wonderful, Tildy—you're so *good!*" Mary Jane said earnestly.

"Fiddle-faddle," said Tildy, nearly poking a hole into what she was ironing. Mary Jane stared at the folds of white cloth. It wasn't a shirt or a curtain or a tablecloth. It had a pretty scalloped edge with eyelet embroidery.

"That looks like the petticoat of an old-fashioned girl!" cried Mary Jane, completely baffled.

"So it is," said Tildy. "Thought you'd be noticin' it before long."

"Whose is it?" asked Mary Jane.

"Belonged to Amy when she was twelve," said Tildy.

"Amy?" repeated Mary Jane blankly.

"Mister Adams' daughter, that is," said Tildy.

His daughter! . . . Mary Jane was so astonished she

couldn't say a word. She knew Ebenadams had three tall sons, grown men like Daddy, who lived out of town and came back only occasionally, but of a daughter she had never once heard.

"I come across this petticoat of hers when I was goin' through the old cedar chest," Tildy explained, buttoning the waistband. "Thought I'd do it up nice and then put it in her trunk o' things in the attic."

"A whole trunkful of pretty things like this!" exclaimed Mary Jane, holding it up to admire. "May I try it on, Tildy? May I, please?" Tildy nodded, and Mary Jane slipped it on over her head. With her hands on her hips to keep the petticoat from falling, she danced a sprightly step, delighting in the skirt's ample fullness.

"It's a mite too big for the likes o' you, though," Tildy said. "My stars, but Amy was a plump and rosy one! I can see her to this day, laughin' little tomboy that she was. And sing! Why, say, that child could sing like a lark from the day she was born. That's when I first come here— there was the two older boys and Amy. Then Robby joined the family, and I'm tellin' you we had a houseful!"

"All those children in this very house," Mary Jane said softly, wishing they hadn't grown up so soon.

"Sakes yes!" said Tildy. She went to the big wooden icebox and took out a pitcher of sweet lemonade.

"We can have a drink o' this to cool us off," she said, filling two tumblers and putting some molasses cookies on a saucer. "Then, when I put away the petticoat, I can show you some other things—dresses and ribbons and such —like girls used to wear in times gone by. Provided you'd care to see 'em."

"Oh, I'd love to, Tildy!" said Mary Jane, excited by the thought. She took off the petticoat and hung it carefully on a wire hanger.

"Today's such a scorcher the attic's goin' to be boilin', so we can't stay for long. . . . Here, drink this up now. Mister Adams says we're due for a storm within two days, and I shouldn't wonder, because yesterday Harryette washed her ear in two strokes, and that's a sure sign."

"Tell me more about Amy," implored Mary Jane, sipping her lemonade.

Tildy put away the ironing board and sat down. "Amy had blue eyes and she could whistle. In them days it wasn't considered fittin' nor proper for a young lady to go round whistlin', and it worried her ma no end. She taught Amy some real nice songs to sing and bought her a piano—you know the one in the parlor—and Amy took lessons once a week. She did splendid, too, but she still whistled better'n her brothers without half tryin'. Come as natural to her as a drainpipe spoutin' water. At last her ma laid down the law and flatly forbid her to whistle inside this house. So Amy used to go rompin' through the gardens, chirpin' like a bird. How it tickled her father! She was the apple of his eye, and that's the truth."

"Are the gardens still the same now as then?" asked Mary Jane.

"The very same, though the trees are a good deal taller now. 'Twas Amy herself that planted that lilac bush by the shed. Least we always told her she planted it. When Mister Adams planted it, she was barely two years old, and to help him out she patted down the topsoil with an old kitchen tablespoon we'd given her to make mud pies with. She took quite a fancy to that lilac and was right proud of it when it prospered."

Tildy took the petticoat and laid it over her arm. "Come along if you're comin'," she said.

They mounted the steep, narrow steps to the attic, walking across the wide, rough boards to an old trunk under the sloping eaves. A five-fingered starfish was pinned to the wall above it. The air was heavy with musty scents and excessive heat, but Mary Jane was too engrossed to mind. Tildy opened the dusty trunk and took out the contents one by one.

"Suppose we should have given these clothes away," she said, "but some way we didn't git around to it.

"Now this here was one of her best Sunday poplins."
They spread out the dress between them. It was pepper-
mint striped, with a black velvet sash and a bodice lacy as
a valentine. "And these was fer school." Navy-blue serge
jumpers and middy blouses with red braid trimmings and
red silk ties. Her spring coat of buff-colored nun's veiling
was there too. "Made by the best dressmaker in town at
the time—a Mrs. Fred Perkins by name," said Tildy with
pride. "Look at them accordion pleats and steel-cut but-
tons, will you!" The coat had a pink crepe lining which
gave the buff a pearly glow, and on the hat to match
furled a pink feather. A faded taffeta hair ribbon and a
round gray squirrel muff lay under a heap of long white
flannel nightgowns.

"See what I found!" said Mary Jane.

At the very bottom of the trunk, in an oval frame of
tarnished gilt, was a small picture of Amy Adams herself. Mary Jane studied it eagerly in the dim light and was
immediately drawn to the friendly little face she beheld.
Amy's lips were pressed tightly together, as though to bar
the escape of a merry chuckle, and her bright eyes
twinkled like her father's. Except for the perky bow that
tied back her long black curls and the old-fashioned
locket that hung on a slim chain from the high neck of
her dress, she looked as young and alive as Mary Jane.

"What happened to her when she grew up?" asked Mary Jane.

"She never did grow up," said Tildy, gently folding the clothes and putting them back. "Amy took to her bed with a siege o' pneumonia. Such a bad siege that it wore the life plumb out of her, soul and body, and she passed away, poor lass. She would-a been thirteen come April did she live but two months more. That winter was bitter cold in these parts; we waited so long for the spring."

Tildy quietly closed the trunk and led the way downstairs. The house seemed still and empty, with silent rooms and lonely corners.

Noiselessly Mary Jane walked over to the kitchen door. From there she could see into the open shed, and at the half glimpse of Ebenadams' bent back her heart contracted with an inexpressible love. Amy's lilac bush stood tall against the doorway, its leaves faintly quivering; while Amy's father, hard at work—almost within its very shadow—was humming a tune under his breath. Mary Jane didn't realize he was mending Mother's broken footstool; she only wondered how it was that, for all his loss, Ebenadams seldom seemed sad. In his house there were shadows everywhere.

Outdoors again, Mary Jane was struck by the brilliance of the summer afternoon. Never before had her eyes seen so clearly; never had they held so much of the world at once like this—from the gardens, teeming with growth and radiant color, each separate petal, leaf, and stem crystal-clear, to the whole broad scope of sky and sun and towering hills. She felt the coarse blades of grass springing beneath the soles of her bare feet and was aware of the warm breeze on her cheeks and arms and legs. Oh, she *never* wanted to go away!

Suddenly she broke into a run, flinging herself down the path with her hair streaming like a mane behind her. Gladness surged inside her like a singing choir of Easter songs.

Though the evening was still hot, supper at the Mac-Gregors' that night was a jubilant affair. Mother's headache had disappeared, and in the three o'clock mail Sandy's shiny Gold Star Badge from Dynamo the Daring had finally arrived. He wore it to the table in all its glory; and, to celebrate, Daddy gave them each a nickel for chocolate ice-cream cones at the corner fruit store.

VII

Ring Around the Moon

THE RABBITS were served their supper in the middle of the next afternoon. Sandy hoped they didn't mind; but, under the circumstances, it was the best he could do. The day was hotter than ever, and Sandy was going swimming at the Ledge with the Big Boys. The Ledge was a deep, deserted granite quarry filled with water, a hike of half a mile through the woods from the MacGregors' house. This was the first summer that Sandy had been allowed to swim there, though strictly on the condition that he was never to go alone and that he had to be home by six o'clock at the latest. In order to stay that late Sandy hurried to finish his chores, lugging out the ash cans and feeding his rabbits, before he left.

Just as he locked the rabbit pens a crowd of boys came rambling up the street, and one of them gave a shrill whistle, to let Sandy know that the Big Boys were waiting for him. Sandy, grabbing his trunks and a turkish towel, was with them in an instant; not without first, however, casting an anxious eye overhead. Despite the fiercely blazing sun, the sky was rapidly filling with rolling cumulus clouds. Sandy crossed his fingers, with a remote hope that the rain would hold off till the next day, but he was convinced that it wouldn't when he recalled the angry red sunrise that Ebenadams had so accurately predicted.

The previous night, before going to bed, Sandy and Mary Jane had gone up to Ebenadams' to show him the Gold Star Badge. A full moon glowed in the dark skies, and wreathed around it was a halo of pale light. Ebenadams told them to count the stars within the circle. There was just one. "Then within one day the storm'll be upon us," he forewarned them surely. "And Harryette knew it yesterday! Tomorrow morning the sun'll be redder than a boiled lobster—you wait and see." To Sandy, on his way to a swim, it looked as though weather-wise Ebenadams had hit the nail on the head. The brewing storm was inescapable.

Mary Jane, at that moment, was coming up the driveway to join Mother, who had come out on the back porch to get a breath of air and do a little more on her tapestry. The plum-colored background she was using went so well with the pattern of pink, blue, and yellow flowers that Mother was eager to see the whole of it finished. Ditto, wearing his red suspenders, was in the vegetable garden inspecting the pumpkins.

There were several ordinary pumpkins and three special ones. When these three were young and green and small as baseballs, Daddy had scratched a tiny M J M on the first, S M on another, and DITTO on the third. As the three pumpkins grew bigger and bigger, the letters did too. Ditto, who knew the names apart, squatted down and traced his finger along the letters of his own. He could hardly wait for fall to come. Then the pumpkins would be fully grown, and on Halloween each MacGregor would have a fat orange jack-o'-lantern marked with his own initials. Ditto checked their progress nearly every day to see that no one made a pie of them.

Mary Jane climbed the porch steps. She was just returning from her first day of weaving at Miss Merrill's, who had invited her to stay for lunch. They were good friends again, she and Miss Merrill, though Mary Jane hadn't explained to her that she was merely weaving nothing instead of doing the downright practicing Miss Merrill had insisted upon. It might hurt her feelings, she thought, if Miss Merrill knew Mary Jane was saving her own loom for the something. Only Mother and Tildy knew about that.

"Well, how did it go?" asked Mother, smiling at Mary Jane's beaming face. "Here, dear, sit down on the hammock with me." Mother moved over and laid her tapestry in her lap. She wanted to hear all about it.

"Why, it's child's play!" said Mary Jane, quoting Tildy. "Honestly, Mother, weaving's a lot of fun and *real* easy! Miss Merrill has a two-harness loom a lot like mine, so that's the one I used."

Mary Jane, elated by her success, described to Mother the way she did it. By pressing down on one of the treadles, every other thread of the warp was raised to form an opening called the shed. She passed the shuttle wound with yarn through the shed. ("It's named a 'poke' shuttle," she explained, "because you have to poke it through!") Then, in order to get a nice tight weave, she brought the beater down against the edge of her work. By pressing the second treadle, every other thread not raised before was raised now to form a new shed; so she poked the shuttle back through that and beat it too. It was as easy as that! Poke, beat, press. Poke, beat, press. Back and forth the shuttle went, from right to left and left to right—at times in perfect rhythm.

"With what sort of yarn did you weave?" asked Mother.

Mary Jane sat forward with a start before answering.

Lightning flared dully across the sky, followed by a low growl of faraway thunder.

"Quite coarse yarn," she said, "so that it would be simple to see if I made any mistakes—and, Mother, it was the prettiest yellow! Miss Merrill made the dye herself from onionskins!"

"For goodness sakes!" said Mother.

"And you know what?" Mary Jane went on. "Those portieres she has hanging between her dining room and living room were dyed at home too. That soft green came from peach leaves and the brown from walnut shells. The red part I knew about already, because Ebenadams told us the Indians used to make red from cochineal even before the white people did. Cochineal's a little red spidery bug that lives on cactus plants. Miss Merrill didn't make those portieres, though. They are very, very old, and the man who did make them wove his name in one corner!"

"Are you going to have her dye your Angora yarn?" asked Mother.

"I don't think I will," decided Mary Jane. "I think it would be better if the first something I weave is just as white and snowy as Polar and Feather and Frosting are."

"So do I," agreed Mother. "Sort of out of gratitude."

"Wonder what that something will be?" puzzled Mary Jane. "I wish I knew."

The lightning sparkled frequently and the thunder growled more noisily, as though crawling nearer and nearer. The clouds were mounting steadily.

"Let's go in," said Mother, picking up her half-finished tapestry. "We have to have an early supper tonight anyway, because Daddy has a Fish and Game Club committee meeting at six." The house was stifling when they entered.

Ditto didn't see them leave the porch. He had picked a red ripe tomato from the vine and was eating it. Popping the last bite into his mouth, he wandered over to the rabbit hutch and stretched out on his stomach in front of it, kicking his heels in the air. The rabbits, who had grown much furrier since their clipping, were listless from the heat. Ditto shoved a yellow dandelion through the wire netting and fed it to Polar. Poor Polar! Feather and Frosting had each other to play with, but Polar lived all alone, without any company. Usually he didn't mind, but today he looked very discouraged, and Ditto was worried. Perhaps Polar would feel happier, Ditto thought to himself, if he could only jump around in the yard. To give his theory a try, Ditto unlocked the pen and held the door open. The rabbit perked up a bit and finally hopped out. He wouldn't jump through Ditto's arms when he held them like a hoop, nor would he run a race. He seemed per-

fectly content just to nibble grass under the sunflowers.

A sudden clatter that wasn't thunder shattered the air. It was the Dump-Truck Man—and Ditto had forgotten to wait for him! Ditto ran out front as fast as he could and stood breathlessly on the curb.

The Dump-Truck Man, in dusty white overalls and big thick gloves, was emptying the ash cans with such vigor that he seemed apart from other humans: a giant immune from the heat. He stood aloft in the back of the truck and looked down on Ditto. "Hello, little girl!" he grinned.

"I'm *not* a little girl!" shouted Ditto. Every week it was the same.

"Having fun, little girl?" asked the Dump-Truck Man.

"I am *not* a little girl!" insisted Ditto. "I'm a *boy!*" and he snapped his red suspenders to prove it.

"You'll get wet, little girl, if you don't go home!" warned the Dump-Truck Man.

"I'm a boy," Ditto insisted. "You—you—LADY!" He had never dared say a thing like that before.

"Ho! A lady, am I now?" bellowed the Dump-Truck Man. "What makes you think so, little girl?"

"I'm a booooy!" wailed Ditto in despair.

"O.K., kid," laughed the Dump-Truck Man.

Ditto couldn't believe his ears. He drew a long breath and grinned with pride. "Bye," he waved as the motor of the truck began to roar. "Good-by!"

"Bye!" boomed the Dump-Truck Man, disappearing up the street in a swirl of dust. "Bye, little girl!" his mighty voice echoed.

Big drops splashed from the sky. A southeasterly wind rustled the leaves and bent them back, revealing their silver undersides. Mountainous clouds hovered like a dark cloak drawn close, ripped by lightning, shaken by thunder. The drops fell faster.

"Ditto!" called Mother. "Ditto, come in!"

Ditto wanted to stay on the porch to watch the storm, but Mother said no, for even that was little protection against the slanting sheets of rain. So Ditto stood with his nose pressed against the kitchen windowpane. The puddles in the driveway grew larger and larger, and torrents of water rushed in the gutters. Ditto wished he was a duck.

Already it had grown remarkably cooler, and Mother

decided to serve hot johnnycake for supper instead of a salad. She let Mary Jane stir the scrambled eggs with melted cheese in the big black spider, and Ditto laid a fringed napkin beside each place except his own. He still wore a bunny bib with long pink ears that buttoned around his neck. Everything was ready when Daddy arrived, and because of his committee meeting at six, they sat down to eat without waiting for Sandy to come back.

"I do wish he'd come home," Mother said worriedly, as a crack of thunder shook the house and the electric lights flickered.

"Sandy won't melt," Daddy comforted her. "Besides, rain'll make him grow!" But they knew from the tone of his voice that he was more upset than he would admit. It seemed strange to Ditto to be eating without Sandy at his side.

There were sliced peaches and cream and cookies for dessert, but no one was hungry enough to ask for seconds. They finished supper in gloomy silence, their eyes avoiding Sandy's empty place at the table, and in their ears was the sound of a swift wind beating rain against the house. The lights flickered again.

"Sandy knows enough to take care of himself," said Daddy. "And one thing we are sure of: he's with the Big Boys and not alone."

"I wish he'd come home!" said Mother.

"If I know our Sandy," continued Daddy, "he'll be here by six o'clock—a little wet, maybe, but none the worse for wear. Rain or shine, he hasn't failed us yet. Count on him to scoot between the drops!"

Daddy glanced at his watch and exclaimed, "Great guns, it's quarter of six right now! I must be on my way."

He put on his raincoat, and Mary Jane handed him his big umbrella. He kissed each of his family good night and said to Mother, "Call me at the club, dear, if Sandy's not home by half past."

They heard the back door close behind him, and soon the car rumbled out of the driveway into the darkness. There was no letup in the storm, and the constant thunder sounded as though a colossal bowler had knocked down all the tenpins in the alley. In less than ten minutes Sandy came tearing into the house.

He was soaked to the skin and his red hair was plastered to his head. His face was so white that every freckle stood out, and his eyes were wild with fright.

"Mother!" he cried in a frenzy. "Mother, where are you?" Tears tore at his throat and he choked with terror. Rain splattered in through the open door in back of him.

"Sandy, what is it?" Mother asked sharply, she and Mary Jane and Ditto all rushing to him at once.

"It's Polar!" gasped Sandy, waving his arms. "Polar's gone!"

"Hold still a second, darling," said Mother, relieved that Sandy, at least, was unharmed.

"Can't! Got to go find him. Oh, Mother, let go of my arm—I've got to find Polar!"

"Sandy MacGregor, you sit down. You're not going out in this storm till you're properly dressed and I get some hot food into you!"

Sandy slumped onto the nearest chair. "Can't understand it," he moaned. "I know I locked that pen. I *know* I did."

Ditto shrank against the wall. He opened his mouth to speak, but the words wouldn't come. Mother rubbed Sandy briskly with a towel and told him to run upstairs and take off his wet things while she and Mary Jane scrambled fresh eggs and heated the johnnycake. Sandy did as he was told. Ditto crept up the stairs behind him.

Sandy barged into his room and quickly stripped. He pulled on clean underwear and his brown trousers, then his flannel sweat shirt. He had to rummage through his drawers for a pair of dry socks. Ditto stood trembling in the hallway outside his door.

Suddenly the lights sputtered for the last time and were snuffed out. The house was plunged into darkness.

"S-Sandy?" Ditto whispered in the dark.

The bedsprings squeaked. Sandy must have located his socks and was now sitting on the bed to put them on. "What is it?" he asked.

"Sandy, it—it was me, Sandy. I let Polar out to play and forgot to put him back. . . . I'm sorry," said Ditto in a hushed voice.

There was no answer. Sandy bit his lip savagely and knotted his shoestrings. Then he rushed by Ditto without a word and fled downstairs.

There were lighted candles in the kitchen, and his supper was on the table. In the wavering light Sandy was amazed to behold the lined old face of Ebenadams. He had come down to the MacGregors', when all the lights went out, to lend them a kerosene lamp.

"Yer ma just told me the news, son," said Ebenadams, striking a match to ignite the wick, "and it's a downright shame—though stewin' don't help none when the damage is done. What's happened's happened, and we can't change it now. But we *can* do our durnedest to get that rabbit back. Me and Mary Jane is goin' with you, soon as you eat up yer meal, and we'll scour them woods, ragin' storm or no. If Polar's out there, we'll find him. Dynamo the Darin' couldn't do more."

The light of the kerosene lamp glowed reassuringly.

Mother and Mary Jane were sorting out rubber boots and raincoats, while Ebenadams put a new battery in his flashlight. Sandy, taking heart, swallowed his scrambled eggs. Nevertheless, it was all Ditto's fault, he thought bitterly, and he didn't mean to forget it.

VIII

Thunder Bird

"TO THE WOODS!" said Ebenadams. He had to shout to make his voice heard above the deafening storm. With Mary Jane clasped to one arm and Sandy tugging at the other, he pressed forward across the field, the beam of his flashlight darting before them.

Already their faces were wet and they could feel the raw chill seeping in between their shoulder blades, though Mother had made certain they were snugly bundled before leaving the house. Sandy had the collar of his yellow slicker turned up around his ears and his sou'wester tied under his chin. Mary Jane wore a woolen kerchief under the hood of her reversible. They both wore brown rubber boots. Ebenadams' rubber boots were black and so high that they reached to his hips when he used them for trout fishing. Now he had them rolled in deep cuffs to the knees of his baggy pants. His shabby trench coat flapped in the wind, and water dripped from the brim of his shapeless hat. His shoulders were hunched and his chin was buried in a maroon muffler that belonged to Daddy. Mother had insisted on his borrowing it.

They paused at the edge of the field to catch their breath and to plot their course of action. The woods loomed before them like a black, forbidding wall that meant to shut them out. Mary Jane drew back and winced at the thought of little Polar lost in its eerie depths. Fearful and unfamiliar in the night, it was hard to believe that the woods had once been a friendly place.

"Let's try the main path first," planned Ebenadams with deliberation, "and branch out from there should our luck go agin us."

"Hurry!" said Sandy, impatient to dive in at once and drag them along.

"Hasten slowly, son!" cautioned Ebenadams. "You're like to miss yer rabbit if you don't."

They ventured forth, three abreast, into the woods. There they discovered that the force of the driving rain was beaten off by the thick foliage arching over their heads, and they straightened their backs with relief. It was a hopeful beginning.

"Good thing Polar's white," said Sandy. "We'd ought to see him right away on account of it."

"But, Sandy, he's probably hiding somewhere," objected Mary Jane. "It may take ages to find him."

All eyes were alert to the wandering beam of Ebenadams' flashlight as it searched out tree trunks, clawlike roots, and clumps of bushes. It circled both sides of the path, and the wet leaves glistened in its light. But no Polar. They called to him, but he did not come.

As the path grew narrower, branches scratched their cheeks, and they had to proceed more slowly. Their feet sank deeper into the spongy ground with every step. They were nearing the brook.

With startling suddenness a spear of lightning zigzagged through the night like a sunburst, and for an instant all was bright as high noon. Then inky blackness blotted it out. A stroke of thunder exploded in their ears and grumbled noisily. Mary Jane clutched at Ebenadams' arm with tense fingers and buried her head. Her heart was pounding with fright. Even Sandy jumped.

"Don't be skeered o' the Thunder Bird," Ebenadams soothed her. "Why, he's a fine old fellow! Wise and excellent, the Indians said o' him. 'Tis the giddy young thunders that do the mischief. Now you just listen close the next time. The first sound is the sound o' the Thunder Bird, and the rumblin's that follow are the little thunders repeatin' what he says. Listen close and you'll hear 'em!"

Mary Jane lifted her head. So long as the mighty Thunder Bird was kind, she'd not be scared by silly little thunders, however mischievous.

"Come on!" urged Sandy.

They groped their way along the brook, calling for Polar, till at last they came upon the tiny hollow that was Mary Jane's secret place, though Sandy and Ebenadams weren't aware of that. Mary Jane herself hardly recognized it. Falling rain had puckered the brook's swift-flowing surface until the little stream was swollen with more than it could possibly hold. Water lapped over its banks, and the near-by grass was buried in pools.

"Why, it's all flooded!" gasped Mary Jane. Her feet felt icy in her cold rubber boots, and, try as she would, she couldn't help shivering.

"Yep," said Ebenadams, turning his flashlight on the turbulent stream. "The waters o' that brook are tryin' to get away from the bed and banks that hold 'em fast. You know, the Indians felt sorry for brooks and rivers, and I don't know as I blame 'em. They said the god o' the river was madder than a snake. Whenever a brook took on like this, they said 'twas he, the god o' the river, whippin' the waters."

"Hope Polar keeps out of his way," Sandy said. "But, by the looks, I guess Polar's not even near the brook."

"We haven't tried Big Rock yet," Mary Jane said hopefully.

"Or my camp," said Sandy. Still, there weren't many places left that they hadn't explored.

Drearily they plodded over to Big Rock. They were cold and damp, and Ebenadams sneezed twice. But Polar wasn't at Big Rock either.

From there they stumbled down the hill and into Sandy's camp, their last resort, where they huddled gratefully under its tar-paper roof. The rain hadn't poured through in more than one or two places, so it was quite dry inside. Ebenadams had to stoop because the roof wasn't much higher than Sandy's head.

"Why don't you two stay here," said Sandy, "while I take a look around by myself?" Ebenadams agreed and handed him the flashlight. Sandy went out alone. He had a queer feeling that if he couldn't find Polar now, he never would. Systematically he searched high and low, under shrubs and beneath bushes, not missing a single chance; he retraced his steps and called without ceasing. But he couldn't find Polar.

Sandy was a sorry sight when he finally returned. His hands and face had been carelessly scraped by brambles, his red hair hung in his eyes, and his distracted brow was puckered. In his heart there welled such an overwhelming pity for poor Polar, lost in this denseness, that the very thought of it made him feverish. Ebenadams and Mary Jane stood silently in his camp. They've given up, he thought stonily. They think Polar's lost for good and always. Well, let them think so! *I* won't stop looking till I find him.

"Now what?" asked Mary Jane in a small voice.

"We'd best be gettin' along," said Ebenadams, taking her arm.

"Not me!" Sandy said defiantly. "You can go back if you want—I don't care. I'm sticking right here till I find Polar."

"Better come along with us, son," said Ebenadams kindly. "Like as not, Polar's found hisself a dry spot where he'll bide till mornin'. He's got a fine coat o' fur and he's in good shape, so our chances o' recoverin' the little tyke ain't so hopeless. Come on, boy."

"I can't leave him here all night!" cried Sandy. "I can't! Oh, I——" KERCHOO! he sneezed, KERCHOO!

"That settles it!" declared Ebenadams. "I'll not have you two youngsters catchin' yer death o' cold. Not if I can help it, I won't, and that's final. Sorry, lad, but you'll have to come with me."

"Death o' cold," Mary Jane repeated to herself, remembering Amy. "Oh yes, Sandy, *do* come home!"

Sandy gave in. He hated himself for sneezing at the wrong moment. Swallowing his tears, he lagged with heavy steps behind Ebenadams and Mary Jane. They left his camp and went back to the main path.

Pictures of Polar flicked through Sandy's mind like the leaves of a jumbled scrapbook: the way he capered so gaily in his pen and how he jumped through arms held like a hoop; his tufted ears and woolly tail; the time he had his hair cut . . . Those were the sunny days, he thought. Sandy was jolted from his memories by a quickening stir in the grass by his side. His heart leaped wildly as Ebenadams turned his flashlight in that direction. But it was only a late squirrel scurrying to his nest.

They straggled out of the woods and recrossed the open field. Sandy refused to hurry, nor did he care how wet he got. He couldn't bear to look in the direction of his rabbit hutch.

The back porch light was lit to guide them home, for the electricity had been restored in their absence. The storm was settling down now to a steady torrent of rain. Mother, with Ditto in her lap, sat at the window, anxiously waiting. Ditto was wrapped in his navy-blue bathrobe; it was long past his bedtime. A pan of cocoa simmered on the stove.

Mary Jane, Ebenadams, and Sandy pounded up the

steps and shook the water from their raincoats like a trio of spaniels. They pealed off their outer garments and removed their boots in the hallway. Downcast and weary, they trooped into the kitchen in their stocking feet. Without a solitary word, Sandy bolted past Mother and Ditto, head turned aside to hide his angry sorrow. He tore upstairs, two steps at a time, and violently slammed his bedroom door. There was no need to ask whether or not Polar had been found.

Mother got up and poured the steaming hot cocoa into the five cups already laid out on the table. She topped each with a thick daub of whipped cream from a blue bowl, but even that failed to cheer them.

"He's bound to show up sooner or later—isn't he?" she asked with alarm she couldn't disguise. "Surely he's someplace close at hand!"

"But we looked everywhere," sighed Mary Jane. It was good to sit down again, and the sips of cocoa felt so nice and warm sliding down her throat that she closed her eyes and tried to forget the whole unhappy search.

"He's apt to have a bad cold, if we do get the little rascal back," said Ebenadams. "Sandy's always been so particular 'bout no drafts blowin' on his pets, and tonight's air ain't no mean breeze."

"Sandy can start looking again first thing tomorrow

morning," said Mother. "If only Polar will be safe till then!"

"Quicker he's located, the better off he's goin' to be," declared Ebenadams, setting down his cup. "Thank you kindly, Mrs. MacGregor; that hit the spot."

"I'm glad. You were certainly grand to go out there in this downpour," Mother said sincerely. "We truly thank you for troubling."

"No trouble 'tall," he grunted as he pulled on a heavy black boot. "Guess I feel 'bout as bad for that boy Sandy as I do fer his rabbit."

Ditto choked. His cup slipped from his shaky fingers and dropped to the table with a crash. Cocoa spattered his bathrobe and dripped to the floor. Ever since Sandy had brushed by him without a glance, Ditto had been gulping down his sobs, crouched behind the cup. He hadn't tasted the cocoa, nor did he now seem to realize that he had spilled it.

"I dint mean to, Ebenadams!" he cried. "I dint mean to let Polar out and lose him. Mama, tell him I dint do it on purpose. I'm sorry, and Sandy won't listen—oh, he won't even talk to me any more!" Ditto sobbed.

They all tried their best to console him, but he wouldn't be consoled. Mother was frantic. Ditto pushed everyone away, kicking his heels on the rungs of the chair and beating his fists on the seat. His small face was mournfully smeared with cocoa and tears, and he cried till he was exhausted.

Mother picked him up in her arms then, limp and unresisting. She held him close and rocked him like a baby. Mary Jane mopped the floor without being told to, and Ebenadams, much troubled by this state of affairs, said he had to be going. He swapped Daddy's maroon muffler for his kerosene lamp, donned his wet raincoat, and bid them good-by. Once more the old man thrust his hunched shoulders into the stormy night.

While Mother was washing Ditto's face by the kitchen sink, Mary Jane poured a cup of hot cocoa for Sandy. She heaped it with all the whipped cream that was left in the blue bowl and carefully carried it upstairs. Timidly she knocked at his door.

"Go away," growled a muffled voice.

"I've brought you some cocoa," she told him. "It's good, Sandy. You ought to try it."

"Don't want it."

"Just try a little, Sandy," she pleaded.

"Don't want it, I tell you."

"It's full of whipped cream," she tempted him.

"For Pete's sake, let a guy sleep, will you!" The sheets rustled emphatically and there was a forced sound of deep breathing.

Mary Jane turned away. She took the cup of cocoa back to the kitchen and laid it on the table.

"Wouldn't he drink it?" Mother asked in dismay.

Mary Jane shook her head.

"He'd rather be left alone," said Mother. "I guess that's the least we can do for him, if that's what he wants."

Mary Jane began to stack the soiled cups.

"Don't bother with those, dear," said Mother. "I'm going to do the dishes right away, before Daddy comes in. He'll be here any moment now. Goodness, how late it is, and what a hectic night we've had! It's high time both of you were sound asleep. How'd you like to tuck Ditto in for me?"

Ditto was shining clean and his soot-black hair was neatly brushed. Submissively he let Mary Jane take his hand and lead him to his room. She opened the door soundlessly, and they crept in without turning on the light. Sandy's clothes were sprawled haphazardly on the chair. He slept with his face to the wall and did not move when they came in.

As soon as Mary Jane folded back the spread of Ditto's bed he shed his slippers and crawled in between the sheets. She smoothed the pillow beneath his head and softly murmured, "Sleep tight," giving his hand a squeeze before she left.

Ditto, curled like a kitten in his big bed, was wide awake. His black-fringed eyes stared into the darkness at the motionless mound that was Sandy. If only he'd turn over and say good night! Ditto couldn't have missed him more had Sandy been far away instead of in the very next bed. Perhaps Sandy would always be mad at him, because he alone was to blame for Polar's being lost. But if Ditto alone *found* Polar—why, then, everything would be all right again. Ditto *had* to find Polar! To figure out the best way to do that, when even Ebenadams had failed, wasn't easy; yet Ditto had his mind made up. He thought very hard, till at last he struck upon a good idea. He'd get up real early and go out to the rabbit pen and follow Polar's footprints—just like Dynamo the Daring found his runaway horse! He'd find Polar and bring him home to Sandy.

Ditto wiggled his toes impatiently and burrowed his head under the blankets. He couldn't get to sleep. It seemed to him that a night spent in his brand-new birthday bed, for all its elegance, wasn't nearly so comfortable as those dreamless nights in his old maple crib. But, no matter how hard he wished, he knew he couldn't have it back again. He was grown up now, he thought pensively, and was supposed to sleep in a grown-up bed. Why wouldn't morning hurry up and come, so he could follow Polar's footprints! Rain danced upon the roof, and away in the distance the wicked little thunders laughed.

IX

Beehive

THE next morning dawned bright and clear, with white sunlight glittering on the newly washed grass and gardens. A brown thrush flew out of Ditto's birdhouse singing a bell-like song. Ditto's own joyous shout rang above the birds: "Polar's in his pen! Oh, come quick—Polar's in his pen!" He was so dazzled by his discovery that he had to count the rabbits out loud—one, two, *three*—to make certain his eyes weren't playing tricks. Last night must have been just a dreadful dream that hadn't really happened at all!

The whole family rushed out of the house, Mother wiping her hands on the border of her apron and Daddy with his napkin still tucked in his vest. They stared in astonishment. Sure enough, there was Polar sitting in the sun, snuffling and bedraggled, but Polar nonetheless. Sandy fell on his knees and touched him unbelievingly.

"How did he get here?" asked Mother.

"Did he come back by himself?" asked Mary Jane.

"He couldn't have done that," Daddy said with a puzzled frown. "Unless he locked himself in—and not even Polar's that smart!"

"I came out to follow his footprints," said Ditto excitedly, "and I found him before I started to look!"

"I wish he could talk," said Mary Jane. "How will we ever know who it was that rescued him?"

"We'll turn detective later," said Mother. "Right now Polar needs the best care he can get."

Sandy took Polar out of his pen and fondled him on the grass while Daddy examined him.

"He 'pears to be all right, except for a cold," diagnosed Daddy. "Feel how damp he is between his forelegs. That's what he uses for a pocket handkerchief."

"I'll get some camphorated oil and the bottle of cold cure Uncle Toby gave me," said Sandy, jumping up. "Gosh, I didn't think he'd be needing that in the summer!"

"Don't forget the eye dropper," Daddy called after him.

"He could stand a good meal, too," observed Mother. "I'll go and scald some bread crusts right away and mix them with warm milk."

"What can we do, Daddy?" asked Ditto and Mary Jane.

"Pick a bunch of fresh parsley, son," he suggested. "That's a fine healing food, and we've plenty of it. As for you, dear, how about getting me a pair of scissors and a stool from the garage?"

When Sandy and Mary Jane returned, Daddy clipped the wool from Polar's chest and rubbed him well with camphorated oil.

"That'll take care of his cough," said Daddy. "Now to administer this cold cure." He rolled up his sleeves and took Polar on his knee, holding him firm in the crook of his left arm, with a finger under Polar's chin. Polar made no objections; in fact, he rather seemed to enjoy being the center of attention. Daddy filled the dropper with cold cure and inserted it deeply into Polar's mouth between the two rows of little white teeth. He slowly squeezed the bulb of the dropper until the tube was empty. Polar blinked his watery pink eyes at Sandy and obediently swallowed the medicine.

Mother came back with his bowl of warm bread and milk, and Ditto had two handfuls of parsley for him. Daddy put Polar in his pen and let him eat.

"If he stays in the sun and gets regular dosing," said Daddy, "he'll be himself in no time. As for your Doctor-

Daddy, he must be off to work."

"Not before you finish your coffee," said Mother. "Did the rest of you have plenty for breakfast?"

"Sure, thanks," said Sandy. "I'm going up to tell Ebenadams about Polar. He'll think it's keen. Coming with me, Mary Jane?"

"Oh yes," she said.

"Me too?" asked Ditto, with his heart in his mouth. In a way, he *had* found Polar.

"Doesn't matter to me where you go," answered Sandy. "So long as you keep away from my rabbit hutch, that is. Come on, Mary Jane."

Reluctantly Mary Jane followed Sandy up the path, her eyes turned toward Ditto. His little face was crumpled with unhappiness. He sat alone on the back steps and watched them climb the hill. . . .

Tildy met them at the back door.

"I have a bone to pick with you," she informed them coldly.

"We've come to see Ebenadams and tell him about Polar——" began Mary Jane.

"He was in his pen this morning!" said Sandy. "Last night he was lost and——"

"Don't I know it!" interrupted Tildy. "Who do you think spent the night in the woods lookin' fer Polar?"

"Who did?" they asked.

"Mister Adams, o' course! Who else?" snapped Tildy. "He didn't have sense enough to wait till the rain stopped. Not him. Back he goes into the cold, wet woods—bare-necked at that—to hunt the little critter. Got him, too, by gum! Found him burrowed under the ground in yer camp, snug as a bug in a rug. This mornin', when I come in, Mister Adams could hardly speak, he was so hoarse. He returned yer rabbit to you, Sandy MacGregor, safe an' sound, but he's a sick man today on account o' it. A pretty kettle o' fish, I must say!"

Sandy and Mary Jane whitened at the unexpected news. Black Tom rubbed against their legs and meowed.

"Can—can we see him, please?" asked Mary Jane.

"To tell him we're sorry?" begged Sandy, twisting the doorknob.

"No indeed! He's havin' no visitors," she stated emphatically. "But I will mention that you called and was askin' for him," she relented. "Now go 'long with you. And be glad you got an honest-to-goodness friend—they're harder to come by than lost rabbits—a friend with a heart o' pure gold, that's what he is!"

They didn't speak on the way home, each wrapped in his own somber thoughts. At the foot of the hill Mary Jane suddenly gave a cry and clapped her hands. "I've thought of the something!" she lilted. Sandy didn't know what she was talking about.

"I'm going over to Miss Merrill's," she went on, fairly tingling with eagerness. "There's a few questions I want to get answered before I begin." And she sped down the street in her green linen play suit as though she hadn't a second to spare.

Sandy scratched his head and stared after her till she whisked around the corner—girls sure didn't make much sense. Glumly he stalked around to the front door to avoid Ditto, who was still on the back steps, and wandered into the den, where he sat down with his head in his hands. Mother's tapestry was on the table before him. Dismally he noted that the plum-colored background was nearly completed. The footstool!

Sandy sprang to his feet. Ebenadams was too sick to finish his repairs on the broken footstool. Mother would surely find out about it before he got better, and when she did she'd be good and cross, because she had expressly said "Hands off!" the day she brought it home from the auction. The footstool would have been fixed in plenty of time if only this hadn't happened. What a pickle he was in now!

Sandy paced the floor and wondered how anyone could be so foolish as to imagine that a rabbit's foot was lucky. Here he had *twelve* of them and worse luck every day! Most of his troubles were the result of Ditto's opening that pen, though Ditto had nothing to do with the broken footstool. That was Sandy's fault, plain and simple. But we all make mistakes once in a while, he thought to himself. He hadn't meant to break that footstool any more than—well, when you came right down to it, any more than Ditto had meant to lose Polar. Neither of them had gotten into trouble on purpose. The only difference was that Ditto had been caught and Sandy hadn't. At least, not yet he hadn't. So what right did he have to be mad at Ditto when he was really no better off himself?

Sandy didn't know how on earth he was going to get out of the footstool muddle, but anyhow, there was one thing he had to do at once. He unhooked his Gold Star Badge and stared at it for a moment. Then he shined it on the front of his sweater and slid it into his pocket. Whistling a little off key, he sauntered out the back door. Ditto looked up at him forlornly, and then, to his utter surprise, Sandy sat down on the step beside him.

"Too bad you have a redheaded brother," said Sandy. "He needs his brains bashed in sometimes."

"He does not!" Ditto exclaimed.

"Thanks," said Sandy. "You sure have a right to think

so, if anyone does. Look, Ditto, I've got something for you." Sandy's hand reached into his pocket, and he held up the Gold Star Badge.

"For *me?*" whispered Ditto. His eyes and mouth were perfect saucers.

"Sure! Why not? You found Polar, didn't you?—same way as Dynamo would have done." With that, Sandy pinned the badge to Ditto's sun suit.

Ditto was ecstatic. Impulsively he flung his arms around Sandy and soundly kissed his freckled cheek.

"Hey, cut it out!" grinned Sandy as he pulled away and rumpled Ditto's hair. "*Men* shake hands!"

Solemnly the two brothers stood up and, clasping hands, manfully shook. It felt great to be friends again, and the Gold Star Badge on Ditto's small chest shone like a blazing sun.

Sandy didn't get a chance to see Ebenadams until nearly a week later, though he went up several times a day to inquire for him. Usually Ditto or Mary Jane came along too. Mary Jane preferred to go in the morning, because now that she was weaving a something she spent most of the afternoon at her loom. She didn't tell a single soul what the something was, nor would she let anyone inspect the loom too closely, lest they guess. "You'll see soon as it's done!" she'd promise, and then shoo her curious family out of the room so that she could go on with her poke, beat, press. . . .

"Letter for Mary Jane!" said Mother, rapping at her door one day while she was weaving.

"From York Beach, Maine," said Mary Jane, studying the postmark. She ripped it open, glanced at it, and exclaimed, "Oh, Mother! Mother—listen to this:

"DEAR MARY JANE,

I'm writing to ask if you could spend next week with me. I do miss seeing you so much. If you can't come then, any week you pick would be fine. I just chose next week because that's the soonest. My father drives down every week end, so you could ride with him.

The water was pretty cold today. We have a new float that's lots of fun. My sunburn is turning to tan now and it feels much better. There is a band concert every night and sometimes we go bowling. I know you'd like it here. Please say you'll come.

With love,
NANCY"

"Just what you've wanted!" smiled Mother.

"But now, more than that, I want to finish my some-thing!" said Mary Jane, quite surprised at herself. "I'm right in the middle of it, Mother, and it's *got* to be done soon for a very special reason. I'd really rather get it done

than go to the beach, even! Besides, it's sort of a nice feeling to be in the middle of a thing nobody else but yourself
can finish."

"Indeed it is," said Mother, well pleased. "Though
Nancy's invitation is certainly a grand one——"

"Well, perhaps when I get the something all done,
then I could go to the beach," Mary Jane figured out as
she slid the letter back into the envelope.

"So you can. Nancy says any time you pick out would
be fine. Perhaps the last week in August would be best.
Goodness me, the summer isn't half long enough for all
you want to do!"

"And I never guessed that could happen!" giggled
Mary Jane. "I'll write to Nancy tomorrow to say I'm
coming but not till later. Now back to my weaving." And
as she closed the door Mother could hear her singing.

The next morning, when Sandy and Mary Jane
knocked at Ebenadams' back door, Tildy greeted them
with the long-awaited news that they could visit him for
a short while. He'd had a fairly good night's sleep and was
feeling somewhat better. Before they went upstairs Mary
Jane handed Tildy a kettle of hot chicken broth with rice
and noodles, which Mother had concocted especially for
Tildy's patient.

Glad as they were to see Ebenadams, Mary Jane and

Sandy were awed by the sight of him. His room was long and dim, with a fireplace at one end between the muslin-curtained windows. Mary Jane's eye was instantly caught by the heavily framed oil painting above the mantel. It was a portrait of a little girl with long black curls, plump and pretty, holding a white-robed baby on her lap; two stiff young boys in belted suits stood behind her. To the right of the fireplace was a massive bureau, topped by a blurry mirror and a crocheted scarf that hung over the edge in tassels. Beside the big bed that jutted into the middle of the room was an old-fashioned washstand.

Ebenadams lay in his bed with two goose-feather pillows propped at his back and a sun-faded comforter drawn about him. His face was the color of yellowed ivory, and he had a growth of white whiskers that made him look like an apostle in Sandy's prayer book. It was a strange thing to see his usually active hands in repose, idle and empty at his sides.

"Well, pull up a chair and pay yer respects, if that's what you come fer," he said crustily. His voice sounded weak and rough with congestion, but the words were those of the same old Ebenadams they had always known.

Quick as a wink, Sandy dragged over a near-by chair. He and Mary Jane both sat on a corner of it and talked to him at once. They told him about Polar and the gardens and the chicken broth. Sandy wanted desperately to mention the footstool, but he couldn't very well do that with Mary Jane around. He cast a pleading look at Ebenadams,

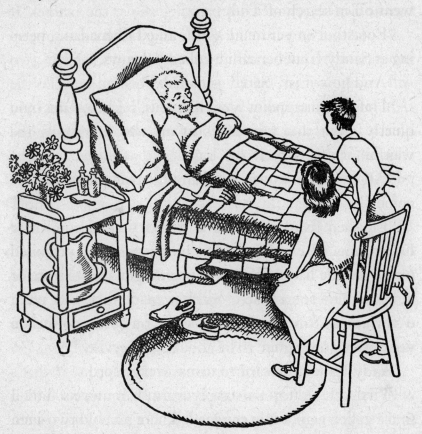

who then turned to Mary Jane and said seriously, "You know, girl, I'm fed up with beef tea and flaxseed tea and all them other kinds o' tea that Tildy pours down my throat. I'd think mighty highly of a good bowl o' yer ma's chicken broth. Right now, I would. S'pose you could get Tildy to rustle me up one?"

Yes, Mary Jane was sure she could. She got up and went off in search of Tildy.

"Footstool on yer mind, son?" asked Ebenadams, peering at Sandy from beneath his shaggy brows.

"And how it is!" Sandy groaned.

"Hate to disappoint you like this," Ebenadams said quietly, "but that footstool's in my shed all ready and waitin' fer you to go to work on."

"All ready!" exclaimed Sandy, spellbound. "How come?"

"Finished fixin' it the night 'fore I was laid up," said Ebenadams. "Remember that elbow grease you promised to use a while back? Well, I hope you got a good store of it, because there's a heap o' work to be done on that piece o' furniture. Now listen sharp, son; you got to do this on your own. I ain't goin' to be about to supervise."

Sandy leaned forward to catch every word.

"First off, you got to apply varnish remover. You'll find a gallon can of it in the shed. There's an old two-inch brush on my worktable. Take 'em outside, boy, along with the footstool—behind the shed if you don't want to be gaped at—that there varnish remover's inflammable stuff and its fumes is plenty potent. Daub remover all over the footstool, and daub it thorough. Then wait half an hour or so, fer the surface to soften up. When you figure it's 'bout soft as 'twill ever be, scrape the footstool with my putty knife—the dullest one, mind you, so's not to mar or scrape too deep. Then wipe the footstool with a rough old piece o' burlap. There's a heap o' burlap by the door in the shed."

"That doesn't sound too hard to start with," Sandy said with relief.

" 'Tain't hard atall," said Ebenadams, coughing. He blew his nose and said, " 'Less patience comes hard. You have to keep doin' the same thing over three or four times —more remover, putty-knife scrapin', and burlap wipin' —till the wood is free as possible o' the varnish, even in them carved crevices on the legs. Got that?"

Sandy nodded; so far, so good.

"Next, on my shelf, look fer the bottle o' wood alcohol; read the labels well, lad. Get a clean cloth from Tildy's scrap bag and soak it in the alcohol. Rub over the whole footstool with it, and watch every last trace o' varnish disappear from sight. Don't be scared if the mahogany turns queer and milky lookin' after the alcohol dries. That's nothin' a little sandpaper won't fix."

Just then they heard Mary Jane and Tildy mounting the steps. "Come back whenever you get that much done," whispered Ebenadams, and abruptly changed the subject.

"This'll perk you up no end!" said Tildy, spreading out a napkin. In order not to overtire him, Sandy and Mary Jane left while Ebenadams was eating his chicken broth. Mary Jane had to pick a bouquet for the living room on her way back. Sandy vanished into Ebenadams' shed.

"Hot diggety!" he said aloud. There by the bench was Mother's footstool. It was so expertly mended that even Sandy could hardly tell which leg had been broken. The very sight of it, solid and firm as before, was like a tonic. Feeling the strength of Dynamo in his muscles, he shoved up his sleeves and began to attack the refinishing with all his might.

In a week he accomplished wonders. He removed the

varnish as much by the sweat of his brow as by the varnish remover; then he fell to sandpapering, rubbing diligently with the grain of the wood until his fingers burned. This took a long time, and the carving made it doubly difficult. The longer he worked on the roses, though, the more he was amazed by the grace of their unfolding petals and the crisp lines of their pointed leaves. Whoever the fellow was that carved them long ago, Sandy thought with admiration, he must have been right handy with his tools.

Finally the wood was so smooth and silky that Ebenadams said he guessed it must be about ready to shellac and told Sandy how to do it. Sandy briskly applied the shellac, going over the footstool without any smears or runs. When he finished the first coat it dried so quickly he began the second one right away. He stood back to admire its sheen and felt rightfully proud of his work. He still had to wax the footstool, though, and he'd better step on it, because Mother's tapestry was within three rows of being done.

Mary Jane's something was growing rapidly too. She often visited Miss Merrill to ask questions, but she still wouldn't tell what she was weaving. Her eyes would just sparkle merrily in answer to their questions.

Ditto gave up. Everyone was always busy these days, busy as bees, and no time for games. He had to make up his own. Ditto collected some crawly-bugs from the garden, put each one on a linden leaf, and gave them a boat ride in the brook.

X

Saturday Jamboree

TILDY knew it first. She told Mary Jane, and Mary Jane told Mother. Mother said, "Now *that* calls for a celebration!"

"What does?" asked Ditto, pricking up his ears. The Fourth of July was a celebration, he knew, and should another one be on its way, he didn't want to miss it.

"If next Saturday's a nice day," said Mother, "Ebenadams is going to come down on his front porch for the first time since he's been ill—he feels that much better!"

"And my something will be done by then!" Mary Jane exclaimed with delight. "It's a present for Ebenadams," she confided.

"Oh, Mary Jane, how nice!" said Mother. "How especially nice to give Ebenadams something made of Polar's yarn, after what he went through for Polar! We can do it up as gay as can be, and you can give it to him on Saturday."

"But it's really from all of us, not just me," said Mary Jane. "If Sandy didn't have the rabbits, I wouldn't have gotten the loom and couldn't have made the—oh, I nearly said it!—the something. Ditto helps take care of the rabbits now, too, so I think we should all give the present to Ebenadams together."

"That's the best idea I ever heard of!" said Mother. "And it gives me a thought." She hastily rustled through the previous night's Boston newspaper and tore out one of the ads with a hairpin. "If these are as nice as they look in the picture, they'll be the very thing!"

"What are they?" asked Mary Jane and Ditto, trying to peek over her shoulder.

"That'll be my secret," smiled Mother, sitting down at the desk. "I'll send for them right away, so they'll be here by Saturday. You're quite sure, dear, the something will be finished?"

"Yes, I'm almost ready to take it off the loom, and today is only Tuesday," she answered.

"Can you take it off the loom by yourself?" asked Mother.

"I guess I'll need a little help," Mary Jane said doubtfully. "Do you suppose Miss Merrill could come over Thursday afternoon, Mother? She also knows how to make things like fringes, and I'd like some fringes."

"I'll see if she can," said Mother. "I should call her any-way, to get her recipe for date-and-nut bars. Some of those for Saturday afternoon would be grand."

"Yummy—what a good cel'bration!" chirped Ditto. "When's Saturday?"

"In four days, dear," said Mother. "Think you can wait?"

The four days flew. Sandy found them barely long enough. On Thursday, when he passed Mother in the kitchen, he noticed she was pressing her plum-colored tapestry.

"Is it all done?" he asked, stopping short.

"Did the last row yesterday!" Mother said. "Like it?"

"Sure, it's swell," said Sandy, turning away.

"With so much going on for Saturday, I don't know when I'll find time to get that footstool to a refinisher," she declared.

"Gosh, Mom, don't rush so," Sandy advised her earnestly. "Next week you'll have lots more time!"

He slid out the back door and dashed up the path to Ebenadams' shed. The footstool needed several more coats of wax. If only Mother would wait till Saturday, she'd have a surprise herself!

With a soft cloth Sandy worked the moist brown wax well into the thinly shellacked wood, covering the whole surface. He had to be careful not to get lumps caught in the carving. Working on it as constantly as he had, he'd grown almost fond of the old footstool. There seemed to be some sense to Mother's antiques in a lot of ways. Eben-adams thought so, anyway. He said, "Fer one thing, lad, havin' antiques is a good feelin', because each mornin' you wake up they're more valuable than they was the night before!"

It took the wax a few hours to dry, so Sandy left the footstool outdoors in the sun. The red-brown wood had a warm glow, smooth and gleaming. Later on he'd come back to rub and polish it and give it another waxing.

That afternoon Miss Merrill did come over. She and Mary Jane spent an hour behind the closed door of Mary Jane's room. Mother and Ditto sat downstairs trying to guess what the something for Ebenadams could be. They knew it must be pretty wonderful because they could hear Miss Merrill bubbling, "*Dearie me, how handsome!*" and "*Good girl!*"

It was the first time Miss Merrill had seen it, and she just couldn't have been more pleased with Mary Jane's results. In no time she had the something off the loom by cutting the warp threads with her scissors and unwinding the neatly woven web from the front roller.

Mary Jane, thrilled with excitement, took the something into her hands. It was as soft and rabbitlike as the rabbits themselves—yet so much had been done with the wool since their haircut! Never had she enjoyed making anything so much as this. Never was there a gift she wanted so much to give.

Miss Merrill said that the warp threads, hanging from each end of the web, were exactly long enough for the knotting of a generous fringe; so she threaded two needles, one for herself and the other for Mary Jane, and showed her how to bind the edge. As soon as Mary Jane caught on to it, she fringed all of one end herself while Miss Merrill did the other.

When they finished that, there was nothing more to do! Mary Jane had only to wrap the something up and wait for Saturday.

Ditto was awakened by the "Brr-ing-brr-ing" of the front doorbell. Sunshine poured into his room, and Sandy's bed was already empty. Ditto sat up with a start. Today was Saturday!

He lurched into his bathrobe and scurried downstairs. There was a big brown paper package on the front hall table. It must have been just delivered, because it hadn't even been opened yet. Mother was in the kitchen shelling walnuts for the date-and-nut bars, and Mary Jane was wrapping the something in a long box on the kitchen table. Everyone had had breakfast but Ditto.

Ditto drank his orange juice and, as possessor of the Gold Star Badge, spooned his Goodwheat while he watched Mary Jane.

"Did you weave a umbrella?" he asked, recognizing the box. It was the shiny white one that Mother's birthday umbrella from Daddy had come in.

"No!" laughed Mary Jane. "But this box is just the right size."

The paper she was wrapping it with was bright scarlet scattered with white stars. Though really Christmas paper left over from last year, she liked it better than any other she had ever seen. She tied the box with a piece of fluffy white yarn which Sandy had spun on his spindle last night especially for this occasion. Ditto pressed his finger on the

knot while she made a large bow, so all three helped even in the packaging.

During the morning Ditto sat on the grass by the rabbits and made three little wreaths for them to wear around their necks. It was most important that Polar and Feather and Frosting have a share in this "cel'bration" too. For the garlands he chose black-eyed Susans, because they looked like baby sunflowers, and yellow dandelions because they were his idea of a regular man-flower. Every now and then he would pause to hold a dandelion under his chin and wonder whether or not he liked butter. He wished Sandy were around to see if a yellow spot was reflecting "Yes!" But Sandy didn't stay home much any more.

At noon they waited for Sandy impatiently. Daddy was back from work and lunch was ready. Mother had promised Mary Jane and Ditto that after they had eaten

they could see what had been in her big package from
Boston.

"Where can that boy be?" asked Mother, looking out
the window.

"Probably coming home through the woods," suggested Daddy, with a knowing nod of his head. "Sandy
always goes out of his way to take short cuts!"

When Sandy did arrive he was flushed and dirty, but
in such high spirits that they wondered at him. Since early
morning he had been laboring over Mother's footstool:
he had finished it in the nick of time.

"Look," Sandy said to his assembled family, "sit down
and listen to a story I want to tell you—lunch can wait."
They could see that he really meant it. Mother turned the
heat off under the casserole and sat down, perplexed.

"What is it, dear?" she asked anxiously.

Sandy stood in the middle of the kitchen floor and
faced them. Immediately he launched into a description of
how he had smashed the footstool by mistake. At Mother's
gasp he stuttered a little but kept on going. He related how
badly it was damaged, how hopeless it looked, and how
scared he was. He told of his visit to Ebenadams and the
bargain they had made. With great warmth he recounted
how Ebenadams had miraculously kept his half of the
bargain; but as for himself, Sandy skimmed over his own

hard work and barely mentioned those many hours of monotonous polishing. He did describe, however, his increasing panic over the rapid growth of Mother's tapestry —that was too narrow an escape to be easily forgotten.

Sandy wound up by saying, "And, Mother, I've changed my mind about antiques—I don't guess they're a rickety pile of old sticks after all!"

Before his family could recover from the shock of this unexpected confession, Sandy retired to the back hall and returned with the footstool. It was a beauty to behold!

Mother nearly wept with excitement, and Daddy was dumbfounded by the splendid refinishing job. Sandy was a lucky lad to have a friend such as Ebenadams, they all concluded. Never was there a neighbor like him! They exclaimed over the footstool till Ditto complained that he was getting hungry.

At that the MacGregors sat down to lunch. Afterward Mother told Mary Jane, Sandy, and Ditto to go up to their rooms to see what was laid out on their beds. They raced upstairs and the fun began.

Pretty soon, with shrieks of delight, they came down hand in hand and paraded around the den, where Daddy and Mother were waiting for them. The three of them were dressed alike! They had on bright blue-and-white-striped jerseys with short sleeves and round necks. Sandy

had long navy-blue corduroy pants and Ditto short ones;
Mary Jane had a navy-blue corduroy skirt. Mother and
Daddy cheered with approval and handed Mary Jane the
something she had wrapped in scarlet paper. Mother took
her tray of fresh date-and-nut bars, and Daddy carried
two ice-cold bottles of ginger ale. They were all set to go.

With a wave at the flower-bedecked rabbits, they
mounted the path and tiptoed onto Ebenadams' front
porch. Tildy had set some kitchen chairs around his old
Salem rocker. Daddy and Mother sat down in these, and
Sandy balanced on the railing with Ditto at his side. Mary
Jane, holding the present behind her back, peeked through

the screen door to see if Ebenadams would soon be coming out. It was half-past two and the August sun was shining.

Swift as a bird, Mary Jane darted back with a finger to her lips. "Here he is!" she whispered.

The door opened and Ebenadams stood in the portal. His tufty white hair was brushed; his cheeks were smooth and beardless. He wore his gray flannel shirt buttoned at the throat, a thin gray sweater patched at the elbows, old pants, and slippers made of felt. His eyes were bright blue flames; he seemed as hardy as ever.

The lively MacGregors, rising to their feet, gave him a warmhearted greeting and asked him how he felt.

"Fit as a fiddle!" he said, but he had to lean heavily on Tildy's arm as she guided him to his rocker in the center of their circle.

Sitting down with a long breath, Ebenadams surveyed Mary Jane, Sandy, and Ditto, who were lined up before him in their new striped jerseys. He turned toward Mother and Daddy and asked quizzically, "No brother 'n' sister suits for you two?"

They burst into rollicking laughter at the very idea. When they quieted down Sandy caught Mary Jane's eye and secretly signaled "Now!"

Mary Jane trembled a little as she thrust the long scarlet box before her. Half shyly she took a step forward and said, "This—this is a thank you for you, Ebenadams, from Polar and the rest. Because you helped us find—well—a lot of things besides Polar. It's a present we all helped to make and—and—we hope it's a present you'll like!"

She placed it in his arms and rushed back to the railing beside Sandy and Ditto. Ebenadams' fingers fumbled with the yarn; his hands were shaking so that he could hardly undo the wrappings. He opened the umbrella box and took out the something.

Eagerly they crowded about to see what it was. Ebenadams held it aloft—a soft white scarf with fringes!

Everyone ohed and ahed and praised it to the skies, complimenting Mary Jane till she blushed to the roots of her hair. Ebenadams took her hand in his and said in his plain, honest way, "Bless you, child dear, I'm much obliged."

Tildy sniffed as though the sun hurt her eyes. She hastily gathered the tray from Mother and the bottles from Daddy, departing for the kitchen to prepare a treat worthy of the occasion. Even Tom, Dick, and Harryette had to have a party of their own. Tildy saw to it that they were well supplied with cream and catnip in the shed.

"Let's see how the scarf looks on," said Sandy.

"Does it fit?" asked Ditto.

Ebenadams put it around his neck and declared, "To a T!"

"It'll be nice for those cool evenings out here on the porch," said Mother.

"And not bad for winter, either!" added Daddy.

"What are you going to weave next, Sis?" questioned Sandy.

"There's so *many* things I want to make, I haven't quite decided yet," answered Mary Jane. "Soon as I get back from the beach I'm going to start either a kerchief for Tildy or an afghan for Ditto's bed."

" 'Fore we know it you'll be weavin' a true MacGregor plaid!" predicted Ebenadams.

Tildy barged through the door, wheeling a bountiful two-decker tea wagon. On top there were frosty glasses of ginger ale with chunks of ice, and more in the pitcher besides. Below there were Mother's date-and-nut bars and Tildy's chocolate brownies and sugar cookies, as well as a pottery bowl of ripe pears, peaches, and cherries.

Ditto gave out the straws and paper napkins, while Mary Jane followed with the glasses. Tildy passed the food around.

"Do you s'pose Indians ate brownies?" Sandy Chief Red Wing asked doubtfully. He'd already put away more than a few and was now considering another.

"If you don't want one, speak up!" Tildy said tartly, holding the platter toward him.

"Oh, I didn't mean that!" Sandy hastened to explain, and helped himself to two at once to prove it. Mother raised her brows, but Daddy grinned in spite of himself.

"Come to think of it," Sandy said seriously, as he munched a brownie, unaware of having done anything unusual, "I'd say a rabbit's foot *is* lucky. Polar and Feather and Frosting brought us lots of good luck this summer."

"And made us happy, too," said Mary Jane softly.